# CAMPFIRE TALES

## ... Ghoulies, Ghosties, and Long-leggety Beasties

### Second Edition

## William W. Forgey

additional
Contributions and Editorial Assistance
by Patrick Sherwood

The Globe Pequot Press

Guilford, Connecticut

Cover Image: © 1999, www.arttoday.com
Cover and page design: Lisa Reneson
Illustrations: Diane Blasius

Permissions: "The Graveyard Rats," reprinted by permission of Don Congdon Associates, Inc. Copyright © 1939 by Weird Tales, renewed in 1967 by C. L. Moore.; "Gold Tooth" and "Predator of Souls" reprinted with permission from Scott E. Powers.

**Library of Congress Cataloging-in-Publication Data**
Forgey, William W., 1942-
    Campfire tales: ghoulies, ghosties, and long-leggety beasties / William W. Forgey; additional contributions and editorial assistance by Patrick Sherwood.—2nd ed.
    p.   cm.
    ISBN 0-7627-0529-9
    1. Ghost stories, American.  2. Occult fiction.  3. Storytelling. [1. Ghosts Fiction.  2. Supernatural Fiction.  3. Storytelling Collections.  4. Short stories.]  I. Title.
PS3556.07315 C36 1999
813'.0873308—dc21
[Fic]                                                                              99-34704
                                                                                        CIP


Manufactured in the United States of America
Second Edition/First Printing

# DEDICATION

This book is dedicated to Ralph, Bobby, David and Christopher
Ehresman—may we always remember our time together
in the "deep, dark woods" and may you continue to have
many adventures in the great outdoors.

*From ghoulies and ghosties and long-leggety beasties and things that go bump in the night, Good Lord, deliver us.*

— Cornish Prayer

# TABLE OF CONTENTS

# ACKNOWLEDGMENTS

My exposure to storytelling came about because of my three scout troops and later many of my friends with whom I have shared the canoeing and winter trails of the far north. I appreciate their enthusiasm for more and more stories over the years. I gratefully recognize the research and editorial assistance of Patrick Sherwood, a scoutmaster who has provided many youth with memorable campfire programs.

# HOW TO TELL, AND FIND, A GHOST STORY

## By William Forgey

In my first book, *Campfire Stories . . . Things That Go Bump in the Night,* I discussed the creation of the storytelling portion of a campfire program—with helpful hints on setting the proper mood, the ideal physical surroundings, and the techniques of storytelling.

These hints were so well received that I decided to share them with you here:

1. The storyteller must enjoy and have fun telling the story. Be relaxed. Do not be afraid of "hamming it up" a little, perhaps at times making a fool of oneself. Being stiff, formal, or even worried about the story will noticeably distract and make the listeners uncomfortable.

2. The storyteller should have eye-to-eye contact with the audience. This absolutely precludes reading a story. The story must be memorized well enough that it can be told without referring to notes or in any other way distracting from the intensity of the storytelling. I probably never tell the same story exactly the same way twice. Get the general facts down and then improvise as necessary to keep the story moving smoothly.

3. Be in close physical contact with the audience. The

closer the better. Avoid standing on stage or behind a podium. Close contact is much easier to maintain in small groups than large ones. One has to make up for distance when the group is large with increased personal intensity and magnetism—not always an easy order. Especially at first, keep the group small.

4. Do not get hung up on details—yet it is details that can give a story its authenticity. Try not to get tripped up on names, dates, or other "facts" as children are quick to notice these discrepancies. There is certainly nothing wrong with making up these finishing touches as you go along. Each story in this book has an outline, giving details of names and other facts that can be changed by the storyteller. I will frequently use names to provide reality at the beginning of the story—then if I have forgotten which name went with which character as the story unfolds, I simply work around this mental block, calling the character by some other description (young man, old man, hunter, prospector, his friend, etc.)

5. Set a quiet mood before beginning your storytelling session. I find that tired audiences are best. Keep your camping group active during the day. The properly constructed evening program consumes extra energy and then quiets the audience down; it puts your listeners into a reflective and receptive mood. This is a must or the storytelling should be put off to some other day. It is unfair to yourself or other members of the group to tell a story when some members of your audience are uncooperative or rowdy.

6. A campfire program is an ideal storytelling medium. It

is the perfect vehicle to use up that energy that young audiences have in such large quantities. As the campfire starts the program should include active participation parts with skits, songs, stunts—all designed to include every audience member. Storytelling by youngsters has to be limited because it can sometimes drag terribly. Instead they can be involved in physically setting up the program and helping run it. Many fine books on organizing and running campfires, with suggestions for themes, can be found in bookstores or at outdoor outfitters. The end of the campfire, after the embers have burned down low, is the perfect time for telling a scary story.

7. While it is possible to have a story session, even a "campfire program," without a real campfire—build one if it is at all possible. Who can not help but feel a mystical sense of awareness when staring at the flames of a campfire? Who hasn't placed a stick in a fire, stirred the coals, and watched the swirling embers go skyward, pondering the mysteries of the universe? With a small group you can allow this. In a bigger group generally you'll build a larger fire and the embers will blaze skyward on their own. Regardless, a fire can play a very important part in setting the mood for a memorable storytelling session.

8. It is totally unnecessary when telling an intense and scary story to use props or to have a secret agent assist you by jumping out of the woods or dressing up in a strange fashion. In fact shenanigans of that nature distract from the basic story and take away from its credibility.

9. Use different inflections of voice to add moments of fear or excitement to your story. Tell your story with intensity and direct contact. At a certain point in the story, when you know that the victim or person in the story might let out a scream, break through the intensity with a sudden shout or scream. With proper timing everyone listening will literally lift about two inches off their seats.

10. Really good scary stories need credibility. A ghost story that features a detached hand crawling along the floor, trying to strangle its victims, might be entertaining, but it will not fulfill the request for a memorable scary story. If you start your storytelling session with true or believable tales, the audience will be held in your grasp, spellbound.

The real challenge then is in finding the scary stories that kids always seem to request. When you do find suitable stories, they generally fall into two classifications: One is the perfect story which helps to set the mood, and the second group includes those stories that benefit from being told *after* a top-notch tale. The perfect story can be told to a group that is only half cooperative, or perhaps a little too large, or too old in age. I would consider a story like "The Graveyard Rats" (or the "Diamond Stickpin" version) to be in this category. Once you have your listeners' attention, then they are on your side. They are in a cooperative mood and then most any story will hold their attention.

Where does one find a good story line? Surprisingly, anthologies of occult tales yield very little that can be used. Generally they are too long or rely on complex descriptions to bring about their effect. And while they make good reading, they are too difficult to remember in detail and tell. But there is the occasional gem.

Folklore books, old scary comic books, collections of short stories, adventure stories, even books of poetry can lend you a story line that can be modified into the campfire story that you were seeking. There is the very occasional TV program that provides a scary theme for campfire use. Campfire program books usually offer stories with a humorous basis, Indian lore, or obviously juvenile stories. Park and recreation department programs are very good sources. You will need to check local county, state, and national parks—particularly around Halloween—to see if they are having a "graveyard" story session. Local parks will also stage programs during local festivals around special events or local folklore legends that might provide very useful story material. Local camps are a fine source of classic campfire tales. Camp counselors are always willing to trade yarns, for their benefit as well as yours.

If the story is well chosen, the delivery does not have to be all that polished. In fact I have tried to include stories that lend themselves well to the telling, and indicate how to go about finding and modifying other stories for your own use.

So come along with me and chase ghoulies from a deep, dark grave; vindicate the misdeeds of a deranged madman; look over your shoulder for mysterious movements in the dark; travel in time to an Asian jungle; and discover swamps with eerie creatures from the night.

# THE GRAVEYARD RATS

by Henry Kuttner

This story started my storytelling career. While still a youngster, I read a story in one of the horror comics that stuck with me. Many years later, when taking my first scout troop camping, the boys asked me for a story. I told for the first time a tale I called "The Story of The Cemetery Rats." It was a rousing sensation. Oh, it attracted no applause, only silence around the campfire when I was finished. But the oldest boy asked if he and the other big guys, who had pitched camp off by themselves, could grab their gear and join me and the younger guys that night. I knew that I had hit home.

Many years later, hoping to find a suitable campfire story, I was going through an anthology of supernatural stories when I came across the original version. Occasionally one of these stories is a real gem and is easily adapted to storytelling. "The Graveyard Rats" by Henry Kuttner, which is reproduced here, is such a gem.

ld Masson, the caretaker of one of Salem's oldest and most neglected cemeteries, had a feud with the rats. Generations ago they had come up from the wharves and settled in the graveyard, a colony of abnormally large rats, and when Masson had taken charge after the inexplicable disappearance of the former caretaker, he decided that they must go. At first he set traps for them and put poisoned food by their burrows, and later he tried to shoot them, but it did no good. The rats stayed, multiplying and overrunning the graveyard with their ravenous hordes.

They were large, even for the *Mus decumanus,* which sometimes measures fifteen inches in length, exclusive of the naked pink and gray tail. Masson had caught glimpses of some as large as good-sized cats, and when, once or twice, the grave-diggers had uncovered their burrows, the malodorous tunnels were large enough to enable a man to crawl into them on his hands and knees. The ships that had come generations ago from distant ports to the rotting Salem wharves had brought strange cargoes.

Masson wondered sometimes at the extraordinary size of these burrows. He recalled certain vaguely disturbing legends he had heard since coming to ancient, witch-haunted Salem— tales of a moribund, inhuman life that was said to exist in forgotten burrows in the earth. The old days, when Cotton Mather had hunted down the evil cults that worshiped Hecate and the dark Magna Mater in frightful orgies, had passed; but dark, gabled houses still leaned perilously toward each other over narrow cobbled streets, and blasphemous secrets and mysteries were said to be hidden in subterranean cellars and caverns, where forgotten pagan rites were still celebrated in defiance of law and sanity. Wagging their gray heads wisely, the elders declared that there were worse things than rats and maggots crawling in the unhallowed earth of the ancient Salem cemeteries.

And then, too, there was this curious dread of the rats. Masson disliked and respected the ferocious little rodents, for he knew the danger that lurked in their flashing, needle-sharp fangs; but he could not understand the inexplicable horror which the oldsters held for deserted, rat-infested houses. He had heard vague rumors of ghoulish beings that dwelt far underground, and that had the power of commanding the rats, marshaling them like horrible armies. The rats, the old men whispered, were messengers between this world and the grim and ancient caverns far below Salem. Bodies had been stolen from graves for nocturnal subterranean feasts, they said. The myth of the Pied Piper is a fable that hides a blasphemous horror, and the black pits of Avernus have brought forth hell-spawned monstrosities that never venture into the light of day.

Masson paid little attention to these tales. He did not fraternize with his neighbors, and, in fact, did all he could to hide the existence of the rats from intruders. Investigation, he realized, would undoubtedly mean the opening of many graves. And while some of the gnawed, empty coffins could be attributed to the activities of the rats, Masson might find it difficult to explain the mutilated bodies that lay in some of the coffins.

The purest gold is used in filling teeth, and this gold is not removed when a man is buried. Clothing, of course, is another matter; for usually the undertaker provides a plain broadcloth suit that is cheap and easily recognizable. But gold is another matter; and sometimes, too, there were medical students and less reputable doctors who were in need of cadavers, and not over-scrupulous as to where these were obtained.

So far Masson had successfully managed to discourage investigation. He had fiercely denied the existence of the rats, even though they sometimes robbed him of his prey. Masson did not care what happened to the bodies after he had performed his gruesome thefts, but the rats inevitably dragged away the whole cadaver through the hole they gnawed in the coffin.

The size of these burrows occasionally worried Masson. Then, too, there was the curious circumstance of the coffins always being gnawed open at the end, never at the side or top. It was almost as though the rats were working under the direction of some impossibly intelligent leader.

Now he stood in an open grave and threw a last sprinkling of wet earth on the heap beside the pit. It was raining, a slow, cold drizzle that for weeks had been descending from soggy black clouds. The graveyard was a slough of yellow, sucking mud, from which the rain washed tombstones stood up in irregular battalions. The rats had retreated to their burrows, and Masson had not seen one for days. But his gaunt, unshaved face was set in frowning lines; the coffin on which he was standing was a wooden one.

The body had been buried several days earlier, but Masson had not dared to disinter it before. A relative of the dead man had been coming to the grave at intervals, even in the drenching rain. But he would hardly come at this late hour, no matter how much grief he might be suffering, Masson thought, grinning wryly. He straightened and laid the shovel aside.

**11**

From the hill on which the ancient graveyard lay he could see the lights of Salem flickering dimly through the downpour. He drew a flashlight from his pocket. He would need light now. Taking up the spade, he bent and examined the fastenings of the coffin.

Abruptly he stiffened. Beneath his feet he sensed an unquiet stirring and scratching, as though something were moving within the coffin. For a moment a pang of superstitious fear shot through Masson, and then rage replaced it as he realized the significance of the sound. The rats had forestalled him again!

In a paroxysm of anger Masson wrenched at the fastenings of the coffin. He got the sharp edge of the shovel under the lid and pried it up until he could finish the job with his hands. Then he sent the flashlight's cold beam darting down into the coffin.

Rain spattered against the white satin lining; the coffin was empty. Masson saw a flicker of movement at the head of the case, and darted the light in that direction.

The end of the sarcophagus had been gnawed through, and a gaping hole led into darkness. A black shoe, limp and dragging, was disappearing as Masson watched, and abruptly he realized that the rats had forestalled him by only a few minutes. He fell on his hands and knees and made a hasty clutch at the shoe, and the flashlight inconveniently fell into the coffin and went out. The shoe was tugged from his grasp, he heard a sharp, excited squealing, and then he had the flashlight again and was darting its light into the burrow.

It was a large one. It had to be, or the corpse could not have been dragged along it. Masson wondered at the size of the rats that could carry away a man's body, but the thought of the loaded revolver in his pocket fortified him. Probably if the corpse had been an ordinary one Masson would have left the rats with their spoils rather than venture into the narrow burrow, but he remembered an especially fine set of cuff links he had observed, as well as a stickpin that was undoubtedly a genuine pearl. With scarcely a pause he clipped the flashlight to his belt and crept into the burrow.

It was a tight fit, but he managed to squeeze himself along. Ahead of him in the flashlight's glow he could see the shoes dragging along the wet earth of the bottom of the tunnel. He crept along the burrow as rapidly as he could, occasionally barely able to squeeze his lean body through the narrow walls.

The air was overpowering with its musty stench of carrion. If he could not reach the corpse in a minute, Masson decided, he would turn back. Belated fears were beginning to crawl, maggotlike, within his mind, but greed urged him on. He crawled forward, several times passing the mouths of adjoining tunnels. The walls of the burrow were damp and slimy, and twice lumps of dirt dropped behind him. The second time he paused and screwed his head around to look back. He could see nothing, of course, until he had unhooked the flashlight from his belt and reversed it.

Several clods lay on the ground behind him, and the danger of his position suddenly became real and terrifying. With thoughts of a cave-in making his pulse race, he decided to abandon the pursuit, even though he had now almost overtaken the corpse and the invisible things that pulled it. But he had overlooked one thing: The burrow was too narrow to allow him to turn.

Panic touched him briefly, but he remembered a side tunnel he had just passed, and backed awkwardly along the tunnel until he came to it. He thrust his legs into it, backing until he found himself able to turn. Then he hurriedly began to retrace his way, although his knees were bruised and painful

Agonizing pain shot through his leg. He felt sharp teeth sink into his flesh and kicked out frantically. There was a shrill squealing and the scurry of many feet. Flashing the light behind him, Masson caught his breath in a sob of fear as he saw a dozen great rats watching him intently, their slitted eyes glittering in the light. They were great misshapen things, as large as cats, and behind them he caught a glimpse of a dark shape that stirred and moved swiftly aside into the shadow; and he shuddered at the unbelievable size of the thing.

The light had held them for a moment, but they were edging closer, their teeth dull orange in pale light. Masson tugged at his pistol, managed to extricate it from his pocket, and aimed carefully. It was an awkward position, and he tried to press his feet into the soggy sides of the burrow so that he should not inadvertently send a bullet into one of them.

The rolling thunder of the shot deafened him, for a time, and the clouds of smoke set him coughing. When he could hear again and the smoke had cleared, he saw that the rats were gone. He put the pistol back and began to creep swiftly along the tunnel, and then with a scurry and a rush they were upon him again.

They swarmed over his legs, biting and squealing insanely, and Masson shrieked horribly as he snatched for his gun. He fired without aiming, and only luck saved him from blowing a foot off. This time the rats did not retreat so far but Masson was crawling as swiftly as he could along the burrow, ready to fire again at the first sound of another attack.

There was a patter of feet and he sent the light stabbing

**14**

back of him. A great gray rat paused and watched him. Its long ragged whiskers twitched, and its scabrous, naked tail was moving slowly from side to side. Masson shouted and the rat retreated.

He crawled on, pausing briefly, the black gap of a side tunnel at his elbow, as he made out a shapeless huddle on the damp clay a few yards ahead. For a second he thought it was a mass of earth that had been dislodged from the roof, and then he recognized it as a human body.

It was a brown and shriveled mummy, and with a dreadful unbelieving shock Masson realized that it was moving.

It was crawling toward him, and in the pale glow of the flashlight the man saw a frightful gargoyle face thrust into his own. It was the passionless, death's-head skull of a long-dead corpse, instinct with hellish life; and the glazed eyes swollen and bulbous betrayed the thing's blindness. It made a faint groaning sound as it crawled toward Masson, stretching its ragged and granulated lips in a grin of dreadful hunger. And Masson was frozen with abysmal fear and loathing.

Just before the Horror touched him, Masson flung himself frantically into the burrow at his side. He heard a scrambling noise at his heels, and the thing groaned dully as it came after him. Masson, glancing over his shoulder, screamed and pro-pelled himself desperately through the narrow burrow. He crawled along awkwardly, sharp stones cutting his hands and knees. Dirt showered into his eyes, but he dared not pause even for a moment. He scrambled on, gasping, cursing, and praying hysterically.

Squealing triumphantly, the rats came at him, horrible hunger in their eyes. Masson almost succumbed to their vicious teeth before he succeeded in beating them off. The

**15**

passage was narrowing, and in a frenzy of terror he kicked and screamed and fired until the hammer clicked on an empty shell. But he had driven them off.

He found himself crawling under a great stone, embedded in the roof, that dug cruelly into his back. It moved a little as his weight struck it, and an idea flashed into Masson's fright-crazed mind. If he could bring down the stone so that it blocked the tunnel!

The earth was wet and soggy from the rains, and he hunched himself half upright and dug away at the dirt around the stone. The rats were coming closer. He saw their eyes glowing in the reflection of the flashlight's beam. Still he clawed frantically at the earth. The stone was giving. He tugged at it and it rocked in its foundation.

A rat was approaching—the monster he had already glimpsed. Gray and leprous and hideous it crept forward with its orange teeth bared, and in its wake came the blind dead thing, groaning as it crawled. Masson gave a last frantic tug at the stone. He felt it slide downward, and then he went scrambling along the tunnel.

Behind him the stone crashed down, and he heard a sudden frightful shriek of agony. Clods showered upon his legs. A heavy weight fell on his feet and he dragged them free with difficulty. The entire tunnel was collapsing!

Gasping with fear, Masson threw himself forward as the soggy earth collapsed at his heels. The tunnel narrowed until he could barely use his hands and legs to propel himself; he wriggled forward like an eel and suddenly felt satin tearing beneath his clawing fingers, and then his head crashed against something that barred his path. He moved his legs, discovering that they were pinned under the collapsed earth. He was lying flat on his stomach, and when he tried to raise himself he found that the roof was only a few inches from his back. Panic shot through him.

When the blind horror had blocked his path, he had flung himself desperately into a side tunnel, a tunnel that had no outlet. He was in a coffin, an empty coffin into which he had crept through the hole the rats had gnawed in its end!

He tried to turn on his back and found that he could not. The lid of the coffin pinned him down inexorably. Then he braced himself and strained at the coffin lid. It was immovable, and even if he could escape from the sarcophagus, how could he claw his way up through five feet of hard-packed earth?

He found himself gasping. It was dreadfully fetid, unbearable hot. In a paroxysm of terror he ripped and clawed at the satin until it was shredded. He made a futile attempt to dig with his feet at the earth from the collapsed burrow that blocked his retreat. If he were only able to reverse his position he might be able to claw his way through to air . . . air . . . .

White-hot agony lanced through his breast, throbbed in his eyeballs. His head seemed to be swelling, growing larger and larger; and suddenly he heard the exultant squealing of the rats. He began to scream insanely but could not drown them out. For a moment he thrashed about hysterically within his narrow prison, and then he was quiet, gasping for air. His eyelids closed, his blackened tongue protruded, and he sank down into the blackness of death with the mad squealing of the rats dinning in his ears.

*And thus ends one of the really great short stories of the horror genre. As mentioned elsewhere, it would seem that books of horror stories would be ideal sources for campfire tales. But, alas, this is not he case. Henry Kuttner's tale "The Graveyard Rats" is certainly an exception.*

*At the end of each story, throughout the remainder of this book, there will be a story outline in large type to facilitate refreshing your memory about the story, even by the dull and flickering light of a campfire. In this instance, however, the following tale demonstrates how the Kuttner story could be better adapted to storytelling for an audience in its early or mid teens. I have found from years of experience that credible story lines have a much more profound impact. In fact when introducing this tale, I often site old newspaper clippings from a New England town as being the source and present it as a factual event.*

*My version of the story "Graveyard Rats" is titled "The Diamond Stickpin." This story emphasizes the evil character of the undertaker and establishes his strong desire to obtain a diamond stickpin that was buried on a corpse. It further shows how greed lured him into the tunnels of the cemetery rats, where he met his doom by backing into the wrong tunnel and being consumed.*

# THE DIAMOND STICKPIN

## by William Forgey

*An adaptation of Henry Kuttner's story, "The Graveyard Rats."*

In New England, which has many towns founded during early colonial days, there are cemeteries that are hundred of years old. Down in the depths of this ground, cemetery rats live. The rats live in huge caves, which they have hollowed out with connecting tunnels throughout the cemetery. When someone is being buried, the rats can sense the digging from the vibrations, and they start gnawing a feeder tunnel. The feeder tunnel is dug until it connects to the new coffin that has been placed in the ground.

They would then gnaw through that coffin—gnawing their way into the body's last resting place, and then they would eat that human body!

Many years ago in a New England town, there was a greedy undertaker. Even worse, the undertaker was actually a grave robber. And what an advantage he had! Before burying someone, he would steal all of their jewelry. If they had gold teeth or silver fillings, he would pull them out. He would take the jewelry from their fingers. He would then remove the valuable stones and melt down the metals from their teeth and rings into precious ingots of pure gold, platinum, and silver. And he would bag the jewels into little parcels of sapphires, diamonds, rubies, emeralds, and pearls.

Over the years he accumulated great wealth in the vault hidden in one corner of his embalming room basement. Oh,

**19**

he had great plans for his wealth. He wanted to retire to a South American country where he could live like a king, with servants, a mansion, and all of the fine things in life that he could imagine. And so he slaved away in the dark funeral home basement, hoarding his precious things, all valuables stolen from the dead.

But greed always has its own special method of destruction for those who harbor it. This man, who was already worth a fortune, knew of one thing in that town that he wanted more than any other object he had stolen. And that item was a beautiful diamond stickpin.

A stickpin is a piece of jewelry that was very popular in the old days. It consists of a straight pin that is used to carefully tack a tie down against the wearer's shirt. Of course one had to be careful not to stick one's self with it, and for perhaps that reason stickpins are no longer popular. On the heads of these pins, people would very often place an item of great value to them, such as club emblems or even beautiful gem stones. A particular old man placed a very beautiful blue diamond on the head of his stickpin—it was worth a fortune, and it was spectacular. The greedy old undertaker felt that he had to have that diamond stickpin!

He also had another plan for stealing gems. In case he did not get to bury someone who had an item he wanted, he would go to the funeral to see if it was being buried with the person in the casket. If it was, that night he would go to the cemetery while the grave was fresh and the ground still lose and easy to dig. Under the cover of darkness, he would then dig and rob that grave. Afterward he would pile the dirt back on. People knew that there was a grave robber working, but they could never catch him. Sometimes he would strike the

**20**

next night, sometimes he would wait two or three nights—but always while the moon was dark and the fog was thick enough to cover his nefarious activity.

The old man who owned the diamond stickpin had a suspicion about the undertaker. When the greedy undertaker asked him if he could perform the funeral service for him, when it was needed, the old man said, "No, you are never going to bury me. I know what you want. You are never going to get my diamond stickpin!"

When the old man died, the undertaker went to the funeral and there, sure enough, in the coffin with the old man was that beautiful diamond stickpin! He knew that very night that he wasn't going to take any chances, that he would have to rob that grave. He wanted that diamond stickpin! He did not want those cemetery rats to get in there and drag that body out of the coffin.

That night in the swirling mist he went out to the cemetery and started digging. He had to dig out the entire lid of that cement vault before he could open it. All of the dirt had to be out of the 6-foot-deep hole. He had to work hard and fast. His fortune awaited him; South America waited for him. All that stood in his way was the huge amount of heavy earth separating him from the cement vault lid and then the coffin.

Finally he had all of the dirt off the cement lid. He lifted it up, straining with all his might. There was the coffin underneath. He took his chisel and he SMASHED the lock off the coffin . . . and . . . then he opened the lid.

BUT THERE WAS NO BODY IN IT. Wait, there was a body—just the feet at the top of the coffin, disappearing into a tunnel while he was watching. The cemetery rats had almost beat him to it! The coffin had obviously been buried close to a

**21**

main tunnel. The rats were aware of a fresh body being buried very close to the, so they had made a new feeder tunnel and gnawed through the cement vault and the metal casket with their razor sharp teeth to GET THAT HUMAN BODY! They got the body, and they were pulling it into their main tunnel.

The undertaker jumped down into the coffin, grabbed hold of the feet, and tried to pull the body out so that he could get the diamond stickpin! He heaved with all of his might. But the rats were huge and powerful. They kept pulling that body farther and farther—he was being pulled into the tunnel! But he was not going to let go of that diamond stickpin!

He had the corpse by the ankles; then he reached up higher on the corpse, grabbing up to the knees, grabbing up to the waist, pulling himself up with the dirt falling around him and the frenzied rats all around. The commotion caused by the thousands of giant cemetery rats grew and grew as they sensed a live human in amongst them. They were being driven crazy with a blood lust and lunged into the main tunnel from all sides. Their frenzy increased as they jumped at the undertaker's out-reached arms, lashing, gnashing, slashing at his fingers, arms, his back, and his legs.

He felt the pain, stabbing at him from all sides, but desperately held on, with only one thing on his mind. Blinded by the dark and dirt, feeling sharp stabs of pain form all sides, he grabbed and grabbed higher on the corpse until HE GOT THAT DIAMOND STICKPIN!

HE HAD IT IN HIS HAND! HE HAD THAT DIAMOND STICKPIN! And he had to back up in a hurry—the rats were vicious; their stench was worse than the corpse's, their heavy bodies were slamming into him. He felt pain everywhere. His little finger was bitten off. His right ear was torn away; they were trying to reach his jugular vein and sever his windpipe! The slashing of his skin didn't hurt as much as the fear that now shot through him, he had to save his life, he had to get out of there before they ate him alive!

Vicious teeth slashed at his nose and the skin on his head. He desperately backed into the tunnel, feeling rats biting at his legs, BUT HE HAD THAT DIAMOND STICKPIN. He backed into the coffin, escaping down the short feeder tunnel, he raised up, BUT . . . THE COFFIN WAS SHUT . . . .

In horror he realized what had happened, he had backed into the wrong tunnel. He was trapped as thousands of rats poured into that coffin with him . . . AAAUUUGGGHHH!

And he died being chewed to pieces by the rats.

The next day out at the cemetery, there was an open grave with no body, the grave of the buried old man. Leading from the coffin was a tunnel. When the sheriff went out to investigate, he realized that a grave robber had been at work and had opened a coffin that the cemetery rats had also entered. There was nothing that he could do about it, but have concrete poured into the coffin to seal it up and fill part of the tunnel.

Two days later townspeople noticed that the old undertaker had disappeared. They broke into his office, and there they found his safe. The bags of jewels and precious metals were inside it. Now they knew who the cemetery robber had been all of those years.

# STORY OUTLINE

I.    An old New England graveyard has been undermined by tunnels dug by cemetery rats who gnaw their way to freshly buried bodies.

II.    An evil undertaker has been stealing jewels and gold from the persons he buries and digging up the graves of wealthy people for whom he does not provide services.

III.    This evil man desires to obtain a beautiful diamond stickpin worn by one of the wealthy old men in the town; it would end his quest for a fortune in loot that would allow him to live like a king in South America.

IV.    The wealthy old man was suspicious of the undertaker and arranged to be buried by someone else when he died.

V.    The undertaker went to the graveyard the night of the funeral to dig up the diamond stickpin, but when he reached the coffin, he found that it was empty—the rats had already robbed the casket of its corpse.

VI.   But wait, as the undertaker drops down into the coffin, he sees the feet of the corpse disappearing into the tunnel, being dragged by the rats.

VII.  The undertaker grabs the corpse by the feet and is himself also pulled into the tunnel. He pulls himself up higher and higher on the corpse, reaching for that diamond stickpin.

VIII. Finally, he has it! But the rats begin biting him viciously. He backs up hurriedly into the coffin, but when he tries to get up—the coffin lid is down—he has backed into the wrong tunnel!

*In telling the above story, I generally SMASH the lock off the coffin when the grave robber is about to open it (V above) and certainly finish with a substantial scream when he finds that he has backed into a closed coffin down the wrong tunnel. The "smash" generally causes the front row to jump about 2 inches in the air, and the ending gives them something really terrible to think about—being buried alive and being eaten by rats, but I do not use the theme of a crawling corpse, and I do not emphasize the supernatural aspects of the original story.*

# GOLD TOOTH

by Scott E. Power and William Forgey

*The ideal story will not only be entertaining but have a moral. Such is the case in this story, in which both father and son learn a variety of lessons.*

One weekend Mr. Simpson and his thirteen-year-old son Jimmy were camping in the Jacksonville State Forest area. They had prepared this camp with very little help from Mom. Well, except for some advice. She saw Dad packing a large can of sauerkraut and asked him what he planned to do with it. He responded that it was for supper on Saturday night.

Mom didn't think that was a very good idea. "I know what will happen," she said, "you'll go to bed right after supper because you'll both be afraid of the dark, and Jimmy will have horrible nightmares after eating that sauerkraut."

"Nonsense," her husband remarked and packed the sauerkraut anyway.

Friday night they went to bed early. Not because they were scared, but because they were tired. They had gotten up early, finished packing, and driven half the day to reach the beautiful campsite that they were able to claim.

Saturday was a busy day. And even though they ate a good breakfast and lunch, the full day of hiking left them starving by supper time. The sauerkraut turned out to be a real treat that evening. It certainly complemented the grilled sausage! And for dessert, banana pudding washed down with hot chocolate.

After relaxing around the campfire a short while, they turned on their AM/FM radio to hear the news.

Unexpectedly, they heard an emergency news report over the radio:

ATTENTION, ATTENTION, ALL CITIZENS:

**29**

JUST HOURS AGO A CONVICTED MURDERER ESCAPED FROM THE
JACKSONVILLE CORRECTIONAL CENTER. INITIAL ATTEMPTS TO CAPTURE
HIM HAVE FAILED. HE IS AT LARGE AND IS CONSIDERED DANGEROUS.
HE IS BELIEVED TO BE HEADING NORTH-NORTHWEST ON FOOT. HE
STANDS ABOUT 6'4 INCHES AND WEIGHS APPROXIMATELY 280 POUNDS.
HE HAS LONG BROWN HAIR, A BEARD, AND A MUSTACHE. HE IS
KNOWN BY THE NAME "GOLD TOOTH." IF YOU HAVE ANY KNOWLEDGE
OF THE WHEREABOUTS OF THIS ESCAPED CRIMINAL, PLEASE CALL
YOUR LOCAL POLICE IMMEDIATELY. FOR YOUR OWN SAFETY, IF YOU
ARE CAMPING IN THE JACKSONVILLE STATE FOREST AREA, PLEASE
LEAVE IMMEDIATELY.

Instantly, Jimmy turned to his dad in fear.

"Don't be afraid, Son. You have nothing to worry about.
Jacksonville Correctional Center is 20 miles north over
Jackson Ridge. Besides we're leaving in the morning, and there
is no way anyone could travel that distance on foot in twelve
hours. Anyway the news report said he's traveling north-
northwest and we're due south."

"Dad, I don't care. I'm scared. I wanna go home, "Jimmy
replied.

"What if I gave you something to protect yourself with?"

"Like what, Dad, a Swiss Army knife?"

"No, of course not. I brought the rifle for a little target
practice tomorrow morning before we leave. But if you'd like,
I'll keep it in the tent tonight for protection."

"You will?"

"Yes, I will."

"Really? Do you promise?"

"Yes, I promise."

"Okay, let's stay. But I'm getting tired. I want to go to sleep.
And my stomach is acting up a little."

Jimmy got up from sitting by the campfire and walked over to the tent and got in. Mr. Simpson walked over to the duffel bags and began to look for the rifle, finding it in the red one.

As he held it in his hand, Mr. Simpson knew the gun was not loaded. And he did not plan to load it either. Mr. Simpson had no concern whatsoever that the escaped prisoner would threaten them in any way. He was merely providing a sense a security for his son. Mr. Simpson was more concerned about a possible bear attack than the prisoner at large.

Walking past the tent to put the fire out, Mr. Simpson noticed that Jimmy had already fallen asleep. Smiling to himself, he picked up a pail of water and poured it over the fire. Immediately the sizzle of steam rose into the air as the fire light disappeared into darkness.

Mr. Simpson turned on his flashlight to find his way back to the tent. He held the flashlight in his right hand and the rifle in his left as he walked. After crawling into the tent, he placed the rifle between the sleeping bags. Once he zipped up the tent door behind him, Mr. Simpson crawled into his sleeping bag, zipped it up, and then turned the flashlight off. As he lay in the darkness, he could hear Jimmy snoring and the gentle noises from the crickets and the bullfrogs outside. For a moment he thought about how happy he was to be in such a beautiful peaceful place with his son, whom he loved so much. Everything was perfect. Peaceful. Serene.

Slowly, Mr. Simpson could feel himself falling asleep and beginning to dream. Soon he was deep in sleep and snoring, too.

Jimmy awoke in the middle of the night, probably around four in the morning. He was squirming because his stomach was cramped and he was having nightmares.

As he lay on his back looking up at the top of the tent, he immediately thought about the escaped murderer. He turned his head to look toward his father, and then he saw the gun between them. Instantly he was relieved. He felt safe again.

Then in the distance he heard CRACK!

It sounded like someone stepping on a fallen branch. Then, he heard CRUNCH!

It sounded like someone stepping onto a pile of leaves. Then, he heard CRACK! again. Another broken branch.

Jimmy tried to wake his dad up, but he couldn't. He tried shaking him, but his dad was sleeping too deeply. Jimmy grabbed the rifle and pointed it at the door, not knowing that it wasn't loaded.

Then outside the tent Jimmy saw the shape of a man silhouetted by the light of the moon. Instantly, without thought, he pulled the triggered of the unloaded gun.

POW!

The gun fired and a bullet ripped through the tent striking the shadowy figure dead.

Mr. Simpson woke up in a panic and didn't understand what had happened. Everything seemed chaotic and confusing. His ears rang from the sound of the gun's firing. He couldn't believe the gun was loaded. He thought for sure it was not. Good thing he was wrong.

Jimmy was sitting still holding the gun firmly in his grip. His eyes were locked straight ahead in the direction that he had fired. He was trembling with fear. Finally he spoke.

"I saw him. It was him. The escaped prisoner. I know it was him. He was going to kill us. I had to do it, I had to do it, I had to do it," Jimmy repeated.

Hours later, the cops arrived on the scene. The man did not look like the escaped prisoner. He had short hair, no beard or mustache, and was wearing street clothes.

Jimmy felt sick that he had shot at someone without knowing at whom he was shooting. His dad felt terrible that he had made the awful mistake of thinking that a gun was unloaded without opening the breech and checking.

Jimmy was arrested as a murderer and taken to Jacksonville prison. There he was placed in the very cell that the escaped convict had been in.

"Kid, this cell is good enuff for ya?" a guard asked. "Ya kilt my brother-in-law, Henry. Well just keep you here till they hang ya."

Later that night a man with long hair was brought in wearing handcuffs and leg chains. The guard laughed as he shoved him into Jimmy's cell.

'Hey, you two murderers should get along just fine in there," he cackled, as he slammed the door, locked it, and walked away down the hall leaving the two in there together.

"Aw, what are ya in for kid? Ya murda someone like me?"

As his cellmate laughed, Jimmy saw the gold tooth shining through the droopy long mustache and beard covering his face. And Jimmy realized that he had finally meet the killer face-to-face, locked in a cell together without anyone around to help. And all because he shot someone he didn't even know.

"Say kid," Gold Tooth exclaimed as he came closer and closer to Jimmy, "I hair you be here fer tryin' to kill me."

Jimmy backed up until he was finally trapped in a corner of the cell. Gold Tooth put his manacled hands out in front of him, reaching for Jimmy.

**33**

"I hates when people tries to kill me," Gold Tooth growled, snatching Jimmy around the waist as Jimmy tried to sneak past him.

Jimmy struggled with every ounce of his energy against the overwhelming strength of Gold Tooth, but he just couldn't break away. Gold Tooth had him and wasn't letting go!

Jimmy knew he was going to die. Gold Tooth was squeezing the breath out of him. His last chance for survival was to shout for help to the guard who had left them both in the cell.

"HELP!" Jimmy screamed at the top of his lungs.

"Jimmy, Jimmy! Wake up Jimmy!" a familiar voice shouted. Jimmy suddenly realized that he was not in a cell, but he was in the tent, being shaken by his father.

"Jimmy! You have been having a nightmare. Wake up."

What had been a great camping trip had turned into a nightmare. But they had both learned important lessons: Pay attention to the authorities when they make an announcement and follow their instructions. Never trust that a gun is not loaded and never shoot at a target without positive identification, even in a dream. And when your mother gives you some advice—even if it's just not to take sauerkraut on a camp out and eat it before going to bed—believe her!

# STORY OUTLINE

I.    **Jimmy and his dad were packing up for a weekend camping. Mr. Simpson ignored his wife's advice not to pack a large can of** sauerkraut as part of their food provisions.

II. Mr. Simpson and Jimmy were camping in the Jacksonville State Forest, when they heard a radio announcement that they should leave the area because a feared murderer, "Gold Tooth," had escaped from the local prison.

III. Jimmy wanted to go home, but Mr. Simpson noted that the prisoner was heading a different direction from them and was 20 miles away.

IV. To calm Jimmy down, Mr. Simpson pulled an unloaded gun from their gear and placed it between them in the tent.

V. Jimmy woke up hearing noises outside the tent.

VI. He saw the shadow of a man on the tent and shot at him, striking him dead.

VII. Jimmy was thrown into a jail cell by a relative of the man he killed.

VIII. The guard returns and throws another murderer in the cell with him, who turns out to be the real Gold Tooth.

IX. Gold Tooth knows that Jimmy tried to kill him, so he goes after him, and begins squeezing the life out of him.

X.    Jimmy wakes from his sauerkraut-induced nightmare and realizes it had all been a dream!

XI.    But Jimmy and his dad learned several lessons from this experience: Do not ignore the advice in official bulletins; never trust that a gun is empty; never shoot without identifying the target; and always pay attention to what Mom has to say!

# MR. BLACK

as told by William Forgey

*This story is an adaptation of a traditional English folk story.*

This story took place in a wild isolated area in the moors of Northern England. One day a stranger came to the village and said his name was Mr. Black. He was a tall, good-looking man with black hair and a big bushy black mustache.

It was the custom of the day that gentlemen would go around the village in the afternoons and court the young women, always in the presence of a chaperon, usually a parent. There was one woman that really took his fancy. Mary was her name. Mary was an orphan child. She may not have had any parents, but she did have four brothers. So whenever Mr. Black came to court, which was about once a month in the beginning, one of the brothers would always be there. They would sit and talk and have tea.

Mary really started to like Mr. Black. He was a lot more interesting than the boys who usually came around. He had been to far away lands, he knew a lot of different people, and he knew strange languages. Before long he was visiting Mary about once a week, usually on a Tuesday. After some time Mr. Black said, "You know Mary, I have been coming to visit you and you have never been to visit me."

Mary said, "Mr. Black I don't believe I know where you live. As a matter of fact, I don't think anyone around here knows where you live."

Mr. Black said, "Well its no secret. I do keep myself to myself, but I live in a house in the woods just north of town."

"Aahh, Mr. Black, that explains it! People around here don't go into those woods. Why I have never been any distance at all into them."

Mr. Black said, "Well they are perfectly safe woods, and I'll come by sometime and take you out there."

Well he never did get around to it, and Mary was just as

**39**

glad. She wasn't too sure about going into those woods. Finally spring came. It was on a Sunday, a beautiful afternoon. The sun was shining, and Mary was out picking wild flowers. She was wandering some and daydreaming. She kept picking flowers, mostly blue bells. She continued wandering along not paying much attention to where she was. Without knowing it she had gotten into the woods north of town.

Now she wasn't really lost. She knew she just had to head back south to get home, but she had clearly gone a lot deeper into the woods than she had planned. She looked around and noticed a little clearing off to the side. She thought she could go over there, get her bearings with the sun, and maybe find a path heading back home. Well she walked, and when she got to the end of the clearing, she saw an old English-style house at the far end.

She thought, "That must be Mr. Black's house. Well he did invite me for tea, and I'm sure he would know the best way home."

So she walked over toward the house. When she got there, she went up the three big granite steps. There was a heavy knocker on the door. She clanged it a few times. It rang hollow inside. No one answered.

She was curious, so she came around the steps, went to the side of the house, and peered in one of the windows. All she could see was a wooden hallway. She was really intrigued by now and thought, "I'm sure Mr. Black wouldn't mind if I just went in and looked around a bit."

She came back around and climbed the front steps. As she did, something caught her eye. She looked up and saw that there were some words carved in the lintel above the door. The words read, "Be Bold, Be Bold!"

She felt that that was an odd welcome.

She tried the door and found that it was open. She walked in and saw a hallway with doors leading off to the sides. Right in front of her was a broad staircase that led up a long gallery filled with windows, allowing the sun to pour in. It was the kind of staircase that made you want to walk up it, pretending you were very rich and very grand. Well that's exactly what Mary did. She walked up pretending she was very elegant, and when she got to the top, the sun was just pouring in those windows. It was all so beautiful. She was still in her daydreaming mood.

She noticed another door at the far end of the hall and thought, "That must be Mr. Black's bedroom."

She walked toward it. As she got closer she saw that there also were words carved in the lintel above it, and these words read "Be Bold, Be Bold, But Not Too Bold!"

She tried the door, and it was the bedroom. It was dark inside. The curtains were drawn. It was a large room. Over to one side there was a brass bed, and right next to it there was a mahogany washstand, with a porcelain bowl and pitcher. What really caught her eye was another door. She thought, "That must be Mr. Black's closet. Oh, he is such a fine dresser. I would like to see some of his clothes."

So she walked over toward it. As she got close she saw that there were words carved above it too, and these words cautioned, "Be Bold, Be Bold, But Not Too Bold, Or Your Heart's Blood Will Run Cold!"

She opened that door, and it was pitch black inside. It took a while for her eyes to adjust to the darkness. Once they did, she saw what appeared to be three bathtubs. The first was filled with a dark liquid. She tasted it, and it tasted like blood. The second was filled with what appeared to be human bones. And the third was filled with hair, long human hair and skin! She was terrified. She ran out of the closet and shut the door. She looked around to make sure that she had not touched anything or left any sign that she had been there.

She ran out of the bedroom. She closed the door and was hurrying down the landing when she heard something! She looked out of the windows and saw Mr. Black striding across the clearing, pulling a young woman by the hair! The girl was struggling and screaming. Mary knew she had to hide somewhere. She looked around and finally ran down the steps, went to the side of the staircase, and crouched down below it. No sooner had she squatted down, then Mr. Black flung open the door. He came strutting across the hallway, still pulling that young woman by the hair.

He started up the staircase, the girl struggling all the way— kicking, screaming, pleading for mercy. She reached out and grabbed hold of the banister. Mr. Black, without breaking stride, pulled out a large knife and hacked off her hand at the wrist. He jerked the sobbing girl right up the staircase, down the hallway, and into his room.

That hand had fallen into Mary's lap! Stifling a scream, she wrapped it up in her apron and ran out of the house, scurrying home as fast as she could.

Well that was on a Sunday. On Tuesday Mr. Black came to court Mary. Mary made sure that all four of her brothers were there. They were sitting, having tea, and after a while Mr. Black said, "You know, Mary, you aren't very talkative. Is anything the matter?"

Mary said, "Well Mr. Black, I have been having bad dreams, and I have not been getting much sleep."

Mr. Black answered, "Well, you know I have traveled the world, and I have read many dreams. Perhaps if you tell me yours, I will be able to help you."

Mary said, "Well Mr. Black I dreamed I was out picking wild flowers, and I came to an old house. I dreamed I went up the steps of that house and saw some words carved in the lintel above the door. The words read, 'Be Bold, Be Bold.' "

Mr. Black sat stiffly in his chair and interrupted, "Surely it was not so!"

Mary continued, "I dreamed that I went into that house and up a staircase and came to another door with more words carved above it. These words said, 'Be Bold, Be Bold, But Not Too Bold.' "

Now Mr. Black's face turned pale, and he said, "But surely it was not so and is not so."

"I dreamed that I went into that door and came still to another door with more words carved above it and these words cautioned, 'Be Bold, Be Bold, But Not Too Bold, Or Your Heart's Blood Will Run Cold.' "

Mr. Black said, "But surely it was not so, and it is not so, and never could be so."

Mary continued, "But that is the way it was in my dream, Mr. Black. And I dreamed that I opened that third door, and there were three vats inside. The first was filled with human blood, the second was filled with human bones, and the third was filled with human hair and skin."

Mr. Black said, "Well surely it was not so, and it is not so, and never could be so, and a curse on him that would make it so."

Mary said, "That is the way it was in my dream, Mr. Black. I dreamed that I came out of the closet, shut the door, went out of the bedroom, closed that door, and was hurrying down the landing when I saw you, Mr. Black, come striding across the clearing outside. You were pulling a young woman by the hair. And I dreamed I saw you come through the front door and start up the staircase, still pulling that young woman. About halfway up, she was struggling and screaming, and when she reached out and grabbed onto the banister, you, Mr. Black, drew out your knife and hacked off her hand at the wrist and pulled her on up the staircase and into your room!"

By this time Mr. Black was on his feet, and he said, "Well surely it was not so, and it is not so, and God forbid that it should be so."

Mary very quietly took that hand from under her apron. She put it on Mr. Black's plate, looked him straight in the eye, and said, "But Mr. Black, it was so and it is so. And here is the very hand to show."

The four brothers took him out back, and they killed him.

And I cannot tell you how, or your heart's blood will run cold.

# STORY OUTLINE

I.    Mr. Black, a new arrival in a small village in the isolated moors of Northern England, started calling on Mary.

II.    Mary's four brothers were always present to chaperon these visits.

III.    Mary is invited to Mr. Black's house, located in the forest outside of town.

IV.    One Sunday, Mary strays while picking wildflowers and comes across Mr. Black's house.

V.    Above the door is the expression, "Be Bold, Be Bold."

VI.    After entering, she reaches his bedroom where the words above the door read, "Be Bold, Be Bold, But Not Too Bold."

VII.    On finding his closet she notices that the words above its door read, "Be Bold, Be Bold, But Not Too Bold, Or Your Heart's Blood Will Run Cold." The closet has three vats inside, which contain blood, human bones, and human skin and hair.

VIII.    Mr. Black returns home, dragging a screaming girl. When she grabs the stair banister, he cuts off her hand, and it falls into Mary's lap.

IX.  When Mr. Black comes courting on Tuesday, all four of Mary's brothers are with her. Mary says she has been having a bad dream and relates the entire story to Mr. Black.

X.  As she relates the story, Mr. Black states that "Surely it was not so, and it is not so, never could be so," etc.

XI.  Mary places the girl's hand upon his plate! The brothers take Mr. Black out back and kill him. "And I cannot tell you how, or your heart's blood will run cold."

# WILLIE BROWN AND
# THE GRAVEYARD CORPSE

as told by William Forgey

*This story is a modification of a traditional Irish folk story, changed to reflect a more American setting.*

nce there was a scout named Willie Brown who lived with his family in a small cottage outside of town in southern New England. The shortest distance between his home and town was through the graveyard. One day his father was taking the shortcut when he stopped to rest for a while. It was only at dinner that evening that he remembered that he had left his black walnut walking stick at an open grave.

His wife noticed that he was looking troubled and asked him what was the matter.

"I stopped to rest today by a newly dug grave, and I left my walking stick. It was the walking stick that your dad gave me the night we were engaged. You know how much I love that cane. I am afraid someone might steal it during the night."

The children looked at one another and thought about those haunted tombs, and then they looked down at their plates.

Willie Brown alone stood up and said, "I'll get it father," and before anyone could stop him, he was out of the house and into the darkness. He walked quite a way until he came to the entrance to the graveyard. Then he followed the path until he came to the newly dug grave. He saw his father's walking stick laying there in the loose dirt. He reached his hand out for it . . . and a voice came from out of the grave!

"Leave that black walnut walking stick Willie Brown and help me out of this hole!"

Willie Brown was really frightened, but a power took hold of him and drew him to the edge of that pit, and he looked down.

"Help me out of this hole!"

Willie Brown couldn't move. A nameless creature, a power from beyond death itself, crept out of that grave and climbed onto William's back. It put one hand around his neck, and with the other silently pointed a finger, showing him that he was to walk away from those graves. William was in a daze. He walked for a while. The weight of that frightful beast got so heavy on his back. Finally he stopped, he could go no further.

"Walk on, Willie Brown."

Willie Brown walked on. Eventually they came into the town where the houses sit side by side—in rows, up and down the street. The rider pointed for him to go into the first house. As they got close to the first door, the monster said, "Aahh! We can't go in here, I smell holy water!"

So they went to the second house. As they got close to that door, again he said, "Aahh! We can't go in here, I smell holy water!"

So he took him to the third. As they got close to that door, he said "Aahh! There is no holy water here." So they went inside. Willie Brown took that dead man from his back and put him in a chair beside a TV set.

Then the monster said in a raspy voice, "Now find me something to eat and drink."

Willie Brown went to the kitchen, and after a while he came back and brought a bowl of oatmeal.

"And where is something to drink?" the dead man asked him.

"There is nothing to drink but dirty water," Willie Brown told him.

The dead man flew into a rage. "Bring a razor and a dish!"

Willie Brown did as he said. Once again the creature

climbed onto his back. The monster pointed toward the stairs to the second floor. When they got to the top of the landing, he motioned for Willie to go into the first room, where three young brothers were asleep. The monster took the razor and cut the fingers of each of those boys and let the blood drop into the dish. With the first drop the flesh color left each boy's face. With the second, their breathing stopped. With the third, they were as cold and white as the corpse himself.

"That is for leaving no clean water!" he said.

Once again the creature climbed onto Willie's back, and forced Willie to take him downstairs.

"Now bring me two dishes and two spoons!"

After he had done that, the corpse mixed the blood and oatmeal together and divided it into two portions. He handed Willie Brown one part and said, "Now you eat this!" He proceeded to gobble his own.

While the monster wasn't looking, Willie Brown took the scout neckerchief around his neck and rotated it from behind his head to the front. While he pretended to eat the concoction, instead he let it drop down into the neckerchief. Then he tied it so that the bloody mixture was hidden in a bundle.

Well the corpse was so busy gobbling his own, he didn't notice what Willie Brown was doing. After a while he looked and said, "And are you finished?"

Willie Brown said that he was. "Then take me back to where you found me."

Willie Brown quaked at the thought of returning to the graveyard. He was scared and exhausted, but he found the strength from somewhere, so he got up and began clearing the table.

He was afraid that the monster might smell the oatmeal

around his neck, so while his back was turned, Willie untied the neckerchief, rolled it up, and put it in the cupboard. Once again the ghostly being climbed onto his back, and they walked out of the house.

It pointed for him to go back a different way, taking a shortcut through the woods. After they had been walking for a while, Willie Brown asked, "Is there any cure for those three young boys?"

The monster laughed so hard that Willie Brown was shaken, then he said "There is none, for we have eaten it. But if any of that blood and oatmeal had been placed in their mouths, they would be alive and would never have known of their deaths. But there is no help now!"

And on they walked. After a while, the monster pointed to a field to the side that had three stone heaps in it. He said, "Under each of those stone heaps lies gold, but no one knows it except the dead."

Willie Brown shivered to hear that for he knew that he was not dead. At least he was not dead yet! And on they walked.

Suddenly the monster made Willie stop when he heard the crow of a rooster. "Augh!" the monster wailed. "Was that the crow of a rooster?"

"No," Willie Brown said, thinking quickly. 'It was only the bleating of a sheep for its mother."

Willie Brown slowed his pace as much as he could, hoping that the crow of the rooster might mean something bad for the monster. Finally they came to the back entrance of the graveyard. They followed the path, but the dead man was getting heavier and heavier. Again Willie Brown could hear the faint sound of a rooster crowing. He thought that the monster might have heard it, so he said, "A barn owl must have eaten a rat."

The monster only cackled as if this was a delightful joke, but then shrieked in his ear "Hurry on!"

Willie Brown felt the grip around his neck tighten and tighten some more. It was as if the closer they came to the open grave, the more the creature delighted at the thought of pulling Willie into the hole with him. Willie Brown went slower and slower, but the creature kept digging its bony knees into his back, urging him on.

But finally through the damp mist, the yawning, open grave appeared before them. "Aahh, Willie Brown. It is into the grave with you."

The creature began pulling Willie down into the freshly dug grave. Willie Brown was so exhausted that he didn't have much strength left, but he held back as much as he could, trying to loosen the tight grip that the rotten, decaying corpse had on him. He struggled desperately, but felt himself being pulled into that grave.

Just when he was most afraid he might be pulled over the edge into the cold mist of the open grave, the rooster crowed for the third time. And the corpse fell into its coffin.

The creature said with its last breath, "Aahh, Willie Brown, if I had known the rooster would crow three times before I had you in the grave, I would have never told you of the gold."

And he was silent. Willie Brown took the lid to the coffin, which was laying on the ground beside the grave, and put it on as tightly as he could, pounding the nails in with the end of his father's walking stick. Then taking his father's black walnut walking stick, he headed for home.

The first light of dawn was just coming into the sky when he reached the cottage. Everything was very quiet. He walked in and placed the walking stick next to his father's favorite chair, and then he fell into bed exhausted. About mid-morning he was awakened by his mother's rough shaking. "Willie Brown, get out of bed. Here you are still asleep, and our neighbors' sons have died last night. Get up. We must go to their wake."

He rolled over and said, "Then go without me for I am sick with weariness."

His mother saw that he was just as pale as the sheets themselves, so she covered him back up again. His mother and the rest of the family left the house and went to the neighbors. Around noon Willie Brown finally got out of bed still very tired and fixed himself just a little bit to eat. Then he headed for the neighbors' place. When he got there, there were a lot of people gathered around, friends and neighbors and family. He walked among them until he found the parents.

When Willie Brown saw them, he said, "I am sorry that I am late, but I have felt very ill this morning. You see, I had a most horrible dream last night. I dreamed that your sons had all died. When Mom woke me this morning, I could hardly believe what she told me, that they had really died."

They looked at him and said, "Willie Brown, thanks for coming. You do look ill. We know how much you boys like to play together. Please sit down over here."

But Willie Brown continued, "Yes, but there was much more to my dream. I also dreamed of a way to save them. A very simple way. I know that I can do it, but I have to be left alone with them."

The parents, seeing that he was as upset as they, felt that this would do no harm and said that he could be alone with the boys, just as he requested.

Before heading upstairs, Willie Brown went to the cupboard and recovered his neckerchief with the blood and oatmeal. He got a spoon and went upstairs. Taking some of that mixture, he put a portion into the mouth of each of the boys. With the first bite, the warmth came back to their bodies. With the second, the color returned to their flesh. And with the third, they were breathing and deeply asleep.

Willie Brown called the parents, who rushed into the boys' room. Then he turned to the parents and said, "Now call each son by his name."

When they did, each boy sat up in bed, amazed to find people gathered around. Willie told them all that had happened the night before. Well, almost everything. He mentioned nothing about that field with the gold. Well they turned that wake into a party of joy and celebration! It went on long into the night.

The amazed and grateful parents asked Willie Brown if there was anything that they could do for him, and he requested the field with the three stone heaps, which he got. After a while he dug up some of the gold and built a house, where his family and friends could come and visit. He lived a long and happy life. But he was always very careful to keep plenty of holy water by the door. And he never again fixed oatmeal.

## STORY OUTLINE

I.  Willie Brown's father left his black walnut walking stick by an open grave in the cemetery, and Willie bravely returned to get it.

II.  A corpse crawls from the open grave and climbs upon Willie Brown's back, forcing Willie to take him into town.

III. They pass two houses that have holy water at the door, but then enter an unprotected house. When asked for something to eat, Willie finds some oatmeal for the monster but cannot find water.

IV. The monster cuts the fingers of three sleeping brothers to catch their blood. Each lost his flesh color with the first drop, his breathing stopped with the second drop, and each appeared to die with the loss of the third drop.

V. The monster mixes the blood with oatmeal and eats his share, but Willie Brown hides his in a neckerchief, which he places in a cupboard.

VI. The monster climbs back on Willie Brown and makes him return to the graveyard. He tells Willie that the boys could have been saved if there had been any of the oatmeal and blood left to place in their mouths.

VII. He shows Willie a field with three piles of stones. He tells Willie that there is gold under the piles, but "only the dead know it."

VIII. A rooster crows, but Willie Brown cleverly tells the monster that it was a sheep bleating for its mother and tries to delay their return to the graveyard.

IX.    Again a rooster crows, this time Willie tells the monster that a barn owl must have eaten a rat.

X.    When they reach the grave, the monster tries to pull Willie Brown into it, but then a rooster crows for the third time, and the monster falls into the grave dead.

XI.    Willie Brown pounds the corpse's coffin lid shut and returns home with his father's black walnut walking stick.

XII.    Willie Brown is exhausted the next day. His mother tells him of the boys' dying, but lets him sleep longer. Willie then goes to the neighbors' home and tells everyone he had a dream about the boys' death, and that he knows how to bring them back to life.

XIII.    He places the oatmeal and blood mixture in their mouths, and the boys come back to life. The grateful parents give Willie the field with the three stone piles. Willie later digs up enough gold to live happily ever after.

*If you feel like writing an original story, how about coming up with one titled "Willie Brown and the Three Piles of Gold"?*

# LOST FACE

by Jack London

*This little known story is one of Jack London's best. The surprise ending, coupled with a scary woodland setting, make it an ideal campfire story. The initial paragraphs, relating to the hero's wanderings can be condensed in the telling, and place names can be eliminated or greatly simplified by the teller.*

It was the end. Subienkow had traveled a long trail of bitterness and horror, homing like a dove for the capitals of Europe, and here, farther away then ever, in Russian America, the trail ceased. He sat in the snow, arms tied behind him, waiting the torture. He stared curiously before him at a huge Cossack, prone in the snow, moaning in his pain. The men had finished handling the giant and turned him over to the women. That they had exceeded the fiendishness of the men the man's cries attested.

Subienkow looked on and shuddered. He was not afraid to die. He had carried his life too long in his hands, on that weary trail from Warsaw to Nulato, to shudder at mere dying. But he objected to the torture. It offended his soul. And this offense, in turn, was not due to the mere pain he must endure, but to the sorry spectacle the pain would make of him. He knew that he would pray, and beg, and entreat, even as Big Ivan and the others that had gone before. This would not be nice. To pass out bravely and cleanly, with a smile and a jest—ah, that would have been the way. But to lose control, to have his soul upset by the pangs of the flesh, to screech and gibber like an ape, to become the veriest beast—ah, that was what was so terrible.

There had been no chance to escape. From the beginning, when he dreamed the fiery dream of Poland's independence, he had become a puppet in the hands of fate. From the beginning, at Warsaw, at St. Petersburg, in the Siberian mines, in Kamchatka, on the crazy boats of the fur thieves, fate had been driving him to this end.

**61**

Without doubt, in the foundations of the world was graved this end for him—for him, who was so fine and sensitive, whose nerves scarcely sheltered under his skin, who was a dreamer and a poet and an artist. Before he was dreamed of, it had been determined that the quivering bundle of sensitiveness that constituted him should be doomed to live in raw and howling savagery, and to die in this far land of night, in this dark place beyond the last boundaries of the world.

He sighed. So that thing before him was Big Ivan—Big Ivan the giant, the man without nerves, the man of iron, the Cossack turned freebooter of the seas, who was as phlegmatic as an ox, with a nervous system so low that what was pain to ordinary men was scarcely a tickle to him. Well, well, trust these Nulato Indians to find Big Ivan's nerves and trace them to the roots of his quivering soul. They were certainly doing it. It was inconceivable that a man could suffer so much and yet live. Big Ivan was paying for his low order of nerves. Already he had lasted twice as long as any of the others.

Subienkow felt that he could not stand the Cossack's sufferings much longer. Why didn't Ivan die? He would go mad if that screaming did not cease. But when it did cease, his turn would come. And there was Yakaga awaiting him, too, grinning at him even now in anticipation—Yakaga, whom only last week he had kicked out of the fort, and upon whose face he had laid the last of his dog whip. Yakaga would attend to him. Doubtlessly Yakaga was saving for him more refined tortures, more exquisite nerve racking. Ah! That must have been a good one, from the way Ivan screamed. The squaws bending over him stepped back with laughter and clapping of hands. Subienkow saw the monstrous thing that had been perpetrated, and began to laugh hysterically. The Indians looked at him in wonderment that he should laugh. But Subienkow could not stop.

This would never do. He controlled himself, the spasmodic twitchings slowly dying away. He strove to think of other things, and began reading back in his own life. He remembered his mother and his father, and the little spotted pony, and the French tutor who had taught him dancing and sneaked him an old worn copy of Voltaire. Once more he saw Paris, and dreary London, and gay Vienna, and Rome. And once more he saw that wild group of youths who had dreamed, even as he, the dream of an independent Poland, with a king of Poland on the throne at Warsaw. Ah, there it was that the long trail began. Well, he had lasted longest. One by one, beginning with the two executed at St. Petersburg, he took up the count of the passing of those brave spirits. Here one had been beaten to death by a jailer, and there, on that bloodstained highway of the exiles, where they had marched for endless months, beaten and maltreated by their Cossack guards, another had dropped by the way. Always it had been savagery—brutal, bestial savagery. They had died, of fever, in the mines, under the knout. The last two had died after the escape, in the battle with the Cossacks, and he alone had won to Kamchatka with the stolen papers and the money of a traveler he had left lying in the snow.

It had been nothing but savagery. All the years, with his heart in studios and theaters and courts, he had been hemmed in by savagery. He had purchased his life with blood. Everybody had been killed. He had killed that traveler for his passports. He had proved that he was a man of parts by dueling with two Russian officers on a single day. He had had to prove himself in order to win a place among the fur thieves.

**63**

He had had to win that place. Behind him lay the thousand-years-long road across all Siberia and Russia. He could not escape that way. The only way was ahead, across the dark and icy sea of Bering to Alaska. The way had led from savagery to deeper savagery. On the scurvy-rotten ships of the fur thieves, out of food and out of water, buffeted by the interminable storms of that stormy sea, men had become animals. Thrice he had sailed east from Kamchatka. And thrice, after all manner of hardship and suffering, the survivors had come back to Kamchatka. There had been no outlet for escape, and he could not go back the way he had come, for the mines and the knout awaited him.

Again, the fourth and last time, he had sailed east. He had been with those who first found the fabled Seal Islands; but he had not returned with them to share the wealth of fur in the mad orgies of Kamchatka. He had sworn never to go back. He knew that to win to those dear capitals of Europe he must go on. So he had changed ships and remained in the dark new land. His comrades were Slavonian hunters and Russian adventurers, Mongols and Tatars, and Siberian aborigines; and through the savages of the New World they had cut a path of blood. They had massacred whole villages that refused to furnish the fur tribute; and they in turn had been massacred by ships' companies. He, with one Finn, had been the sole survivors of such a company. They had spent a winter of solitude and starvation on a lonely Aleutian isle, and their rescue in the spring by another fur ship had been one chance in a thousand.

But always the terrible savagery had hemmed him in. Passing from ship to ship, and ever refusing to return, he had come to the ship that explored the south. All down the

Alaskan coast they had encountered nothing but hosts of savages. Every anchorage among the beetling islands or under the frowning cliffs of the mainland had meant a battle or a storm. Either the gales blew, threatening destruction, or the war canoes came off, manned by howling natives with the war paint on their faces, who came to learn the bloody virtues of the sea rovers' gunpowder. South, south they had coasted, clear to the myth land of California. Here, it was said, were Spanish adventurers who had fought their way up from Mexico. He had had hopes of those Spanish adventurers. Escaping to them, the rest would have been easy—a year or two, what did it matter more or less?—and he would win to Mexico, then a ship, and Europe would be his. But they had met no Spaniards. Only had they encountered the same impregnable wall of savagery. The denizens of the confines of the world, painted for war, had driven them back from the shores. At last, when one boat was cut off and every man killed, the commander had abandoned the quest and sailed back to the North.

The years had passed. He had served under Tebenkoff when Michaelovski Redoubt was built. He had spent two years in the Kuskokwim country. Two summers, in the month of June, he had managed to be at the head of Kotzebue Sound. Here, at this time, the tribes assembled for barter; here were to be found spotted deerskins from Siberia, ivory from the Diomedes, walrus skins from the shores of the Arctic, strange stone lamps, passing in trade from tribe to tribe, no one knew whence, and once, a hunting knife of English make; and here, Subienkow knew, was the school in which to learn geography. For he met Eskimos from Norton Sound, from King Island and St. Lawrence Island, from Cape Prince of

**65**

Wales, and Point Barrow. Such places had other names, and
their distances were measured in days.

It was a vast region these trading savages came from, and a
vaster region from which, by repeated trade, their stone lamps
and that steel knife had come. Subienkow bullied and cajoled
and bribed. Every far journeyer or strange tribesman was
brought before him. Perils unaccountable and unthinkable
were mentioned, as well as wild beasts, hostile tribes, impene-
trable forests, and mighty mountain ranges; but always from
beyond came the rumor and the tale of white-skinned men,
blue of eye and fair of hair, who fought like devils and who
sought always for furs. They were to the east—far, far to the
east. No one had seen them. It was the word that had been
passed along.

It was a hard school. One could not learn geography very
well through the medium of strange dialects, from dark minds
that mingled fact and fable and that measured distances by
"sleeps" that varied according to the difficulty of the going.
But at last came the whisper that gave Subienkow courage. In
the east lay a great river where were these blue-eyed men. The
river was called the Yukon. South of Michaelovski Redoubt
emptied another great river which the Russians knew as the
Kwikpak. These two rivers were one, ran the whisper.

Subienkow returned to Michaelovski. For a year he urged
an expedition up the Kwikpak. Then arose Malakoff, the
Russian half-breed, to lead the wildest and most ferocious of
the hell's broth of mongrel adventurers who had crossed from
Kamchatka. Subienkow was his lieutenant. They threaded the
mazes of the great delta of the Kwikpak, picked up the first
low hills on the northern bank, and for half a thousand miles,
in skin canoes loaded to the gunwales with trade goods and

ammunition, fought their way against the five-knot current of a river that ran from two to ten miles wide in a channel many fathoms deep. Malakoff decided to build the fort at Nulato. Subienkow urged to go farther. But he quickly reconciled himself to Nulato. The long winter was coming on. It would be better to wait. Early the following summer, when the ice was gone, he would disappear up the Kwikpak and work his way to the Hudson's Bay Company's posts. Malakoff had never heard the whisper that the Kwikpak was the Yukon, and Subienkow did not tell him.

Came the building of the fort. It was enforced labor. The tiered walls of logs arose to the sighs and groans of the Nulato Indians. The lash was laid upon their backs, and it was the iron hand of the freebooters of the sea that laid on the lash. There were Indians that ran away, and when they were caught they were brought back and spread-eagled before the fort, where they and their tribe learned the efficacy of the knout. Two died under it; others were injured for life; and the rest took the lesson to heart and ran away no more. The snow was flying ere the fort was finished, and then it was the time for furs. A heavy tribute was laid upon the tribe. Blows and lash-ings continued, and that the tribute should be paid, the women and children were held as hostages and treated with the barbarity that only the fur thieves knew.

Well, it had been a sowing of blood, and now was come the harvest. The fort was gone. In the light of its burning, half the fur thieves had been cut down. The other half had passed under the torture. Only Subienkow remained, or Subienkow and Big Ivan, if that whimpering, moaning thing in the snow could be called Big Ivan. Subienkow caught Yakaga grinning at him. There was no gainsaying Yakaga. The mark of the lash was still on his face. After all, Subienkow could not blame him, but he disliked the thought of what Yakaga would do to him. He thought of appealing to Makamuk, the head chief; but his judgment told him that such appeal was useless. Then, too, he thought of bursting his bonds and dying fighting. Such an end would be quick. But he could not break his bonds. Caribou thongs were stronger than he. Still devising, another thought came to him. He signed for Makamuk, and that an interpreter who knew the coast dialect should be brought.

"Oh, Makamuk," he said, "I am not minded to die, I am a great man, and it were foolishness for me to die. In truth, I shall not die. I am not like these other carrion."

He looked at the moaning thing that had once been Big Ivan, and stirred it contemptuously with his toe.

"I am too wise to die. Behold, I have a great medicine. I alone know this medicine. Since I am not going to die, I shall exchange this medicine with you."

"What is this medicine?" Makamuk demanded.

"It is a strange medicine."

Subienkow debated with himself for a moment, as if loath to part with the secret.

"I will tell you. A little bit of this medicine rubbed on the skin makes the skin hard like a rock, hard like iron, so that no cutting weapon can cut it. The strongest blow of a cutting weapon is a vain thing against it. A bone knife becomes like a piece of mud; and it will turn the edge of the iron knives we have brought among you. What will you give me for the secret of the medicine?"

"I will give you your life," Makamuk made answer through the interpreter.

Subienkow laughed scornfully.

"And you shall be a slave in my house until you die."

The Pole laughed more scornfully.

"Untie my hands and feet and let us talk," he said.

The chief made the sign; and when he was loosed Subienkow rolled a cigarette and lighted it.

"This is foolish talk," said Makamuk. "There is no such medicine. It cannot be. A cutting edge is stronger than any medicine."

The chief was incredulous, and yet he wavered. He had seen too many deviltries of fur thieves that worked. He could not wholly doubt.

"I will give you your life; but you shall not be a slave," he announced.

"More than that."

Subienkow played his game as coolly as if he were bartering for a fox skin.

"It is a very great medicine. It has saved my life many times. I want a sled and dogs, and six of your hunters to travel with me down the river and give me safety to one day's sleep from Michaelovski Redoubt.

"You must live here, and teach us all of your deviltries," was the reply.

Subienkow shrugged his shoulders and remained silent. He blew cigarette smoke out on the icy air, and curiously regarded what remained of the big Cossack.

"That scar!" Makamuk said suddenly, pointing to the Pole's neck, where a livid mark advertised the slash of a knife in a Kamchatkan brawl. "The medicine is not good. The cutting edge was stronger than the medicine."

"It was a strong man that drove the stroke." (Subienkow

considered.)

"Stronger than you, stronger than your strongest hunter, stronger than he."

Again, with the toe of his moccasin, he touched the Cossack—a grisly spectacle, no longer conscious—yet in whose dismembered body the pain-racked life clung and was loath to go.

"Also the medicine was weak. For at that place there were no berries of a certain kind, of which I see you have plenty in this country. The medicine here will be strong."

"I will let you go down river," said Makamuk, "and the sled and the dogs and the six hunters to give you safety shall be yours."

"You are slow," was the cool rejoinder. "You have committed an offense against my medicine in that you did not at once accept my terms. Behold, I now demand more. I want one hundred beaver skins." (Makamuk sneered.) "I want one hundred pounds of dried fish." (Makamuk nodded, for fish were plentiful and cheap.) "I want two sleds—one for me and one for my furs and fish. And my rifle must be returned to me. If you do not like the price, in a little while the price will grow."

Yakaga whispered to the chief.

"But how can I know your medicine is true medicine?" Makamuk asked.

"It is very easy. First, I shall go into the woods—"

Again Yakaga whispered to Makamuk, who made a suspicious dissent.

"You can send twenty hunters with me," Subienkow went on. "You see, I must get the berries and the roots with which to make the medicine. Then, when you have brought the two sleds and loaded on them the fish and the beaver skins and the rifle, and when you have told off the six hunters who will go with me—then, when all is ready, I will rub the medicine on my neck, so, and lay my neck there on that log. Then can your strongest hunter take the ax and strike three times on my neck. You yourself can strike the first three times.

Makamuk stood with gaping mouth, drinking in this latest and most wonderful magic of the fur thieves.

"But first," the Pole added hastily, "between each blow I must put on fresh medicine. The ax is heavy and sharp, and I want no mistakes."

"All that you have asked shall be yours," Makamuk cried in a rush of acceptance. "Proceed to make your medicine."

Subienkow concealed his elation. He was playing a desperate game, and there must be no slips. He spoke arrogantly.

"You have been slow. My medicine is offended. To make the offense clean you must give me your daughter."

He pointed to the girl, an unwholesome creature, with a cast in one eye and a bristling wolf tooth. Makamuk was angry, but the Pole remained imperturbable, rolling and lighting another cigarette.

"Make haste," he threatened. "If you are not quick, I shall demand yet more."

In the silence that followed, the dreary Northland scene faded from before him, and he saw once more his native land, and France, and once, as he glanced at the wolf-toothed girl, he remembered another girl, a singer and a dancer, whom he had known when first as a youth he came to Paris.

"What do you want with the girl?" Makamuk asked.

"To go down the river with me." Subienkow glanced her over critically. "She will make a good wife, and it is an honor worthy of my medicine to be married to your blood."

Again he remembered the singer and dancer and hummed aloud a song she had taught him. He lived the old life over, but in a detached, impersonal sort of way, looking at the memory pictures of his own life as if they were pictures in a book of anybody's life. The chief's voice, abruptly breaking the silence, startled him.

"It shall be done," said Makamuk. "The girl shall go down the river with you. But be it understood that I myself strike the three blows with the ax on your neck."

"But each time I shall put on the medicine," Subienkow answered, with a show of ill-concealed anxiety.

"You shall put the medicine on between each blow. Here are the hunters who shall see you do not escape. Go into the forest and gather your medicine."

Makamuk had been convinced of the worth of the medicine by the Pole's rapacity. Surely nothing less than the greatest of medicines could enable a man in the shadow of death to stand up and drive an old woman's bargain.

"Besides," whispered Yakaga, when the Pole, with this guard, had disappeared among the spruce trees, "when you have learned the medicine you can easily destroy him."

"There will be some part where he has not rubbed the medicine," was Yakaga's reply. "We will destroy him through that part. It may be his ears. Very well; we will thrust a spear in one ear and out the other. Or it may be his eyes. Surely the medicine will be much too strong to rub on his eyes."

The chief nodded. "You are wise, Yakaga. If he possesses no other devil things, we will then destroy him."

Subienkow did not waste time in gathering the ingredients for his medicine. He selected whatsoever came to hand such as spruce needles, the inner bark of the willow, a strip of birch bark, and a quantity of mossberries, which he made the hunters dig up for him from beneath the snow. A few frozen roots completed his supply, and he led the way back to camp.

Makamuk and Yakaga crouched beside him, noting the quantities and kinds of the ingredients he dropped into the pot of boiling water.

"You must be careful that the mossberries go in first," he explained.

"And—of yes, one other thing—the finger of a man. Here, Yakaga, let me cut off your finger."

But Yakaga put his hands behind him and scowled.

"Just a small finger," Subienkow pleaded.

"Yakaga, give him your finger," Makamuk commanded.

"There be plenty of fingers lying around," Yakaga grunted, indicating the human wreckage in the snow of the score of persons who had been tortured to death.

"It must be the finger of a live man," the Pole objected.

"Then shall you have the finger of a live man." Yakaga strode over to the Cossack and sliced off a finger.

"He is not yet dead," he announced, flinging the bloody trophy in the snow at the Pole's feet, "Also, it is a good finger, because it is large."

Subienkow dropped it into the fire under the pot and began to sing. It was a French love song that with great solemnity he sang into the brew.

"Without these words I utter into it the medicine is worthless," he explained. "The words are the chiefest strength of it. Behold, it is ready."

"Name the words slowly, that I may know them," Makamuk commanded.

"Not until after the test. When the ax flies back three times from my neck, then will I give you the secret of the words."

"But if the medicine is not good medicine?" Makamuk queried anxiously.

Subienkow turned upon him wrathfully.

"My medicine is always good. However, if it is not good, then do by me as you have done to the others. Cut me up a bit at a time, even as you have cut him up." He pointed to Cossack. "The medicine is now cool. Thus I rub it on my neck, saying this further medicine."

With great gravity he slowly intoned a line of the "Marseillaise," at the same time rubbing the villainous brew thoroughly into his neck.

An outcry interrupted his play acting. The giant Cossack, with a last resurgence of his tremendous vitality, had arisen to his knees. Laughter and cries of surprise and applause arose from the Nulatos, as Big Ivan began flinging himself about in the snow with mighty spasms.

Subienkow was made sick by the sight, but he mastered his qualms and made believe to be angry.

"This will not do," he said. "Finish him, and then we will make the test. Here, you, Yakaga, see that his noise ceases."

While this was being done, Subienkow turned to Makamuk.

"And remember, you are to strike hard. This is not baby work. Here, take the ax and strike the log, so I can see you strike like a man."

Makamuk obeyed, striking twice, precisely and with vigor, cutting out a large chip.

"It is well." Subienkow looked about him at the circle of savage faces that somehow seemed to symbolize the wall of savagery that had hemmed him about ever since the Czar's police had first arrested him in Warsaw. "Take your ax, Makamuk, and stand so. I shall lie down. When I raise my hand, strike, and strike with all your might. And be careful that no one stands behind you. The medicine is good, and the ax may bounce from off my neck and right out of your hands."

He looked at the two sleds, with the dogs in harness, loaded with furs and fish. His rifle lay on top of the beaver skins. The six hunters who were to act as his guard stood by the sleds.

"Where is the girl?" the Pole demanded. "Bring her up to the sleds before the test goes on."

When this had been carried out, Subienkow lay down in the snow, resting his head on the log like a tired child about to sleep. He had lived so many dreary years that he was indeed tired.

"I laugh at you and your strength, O Makamuk," he said. "Strike, and strike hard."

He lifted his hand. Makamuk swung the ax, a broadax for the squaring of logs. The bright steel flashed through the frosty air, poised for a perceptible instant above Makamuk's head, then descended upon Subienkow's bare neck. Clear through flesh and bone it cut its way, biting deeply into the log beneath. The amazed savages saw the head bounce a yard away from the blood-spouting trunk.

There was a great bewilderment and silence, while slowly it began to dawn in their minds that there had been no medicine. The fur thief had outwitted them. Alone, of all their prisoners, he had escaped the torture. That had been the stake for which he played. A great roar of laughter went up. Makamuk bowed his head in shame. The fur thief had fooled him. He

**75**

had lost face before all his people. Still they continued to roar out their laughter. Makamuk turned, and with bowed head stalked away. He knew that thenceforth he would be no longer known as Makamuk. He would be Lost Face; the record of his shame would be with him until he died; and whenever the tribes gathered in the spring for the salmon, or in the summer for the trading, the story would pass back and forth across the campfires of how the fur thief died peaceably, at a single stroke, by the hand of Lost Face.

"Who was Lost Face?" he could hear, in anticipation, some insolent young buck demand. "Oh, Lost Face," would be the answer, "he who once was Makamuk in the days before he cut off the fur thief's head."

# STORY OUTLINE

I.  Subienkow was a Polish adventurer who had escaped from Poland across Siberia, after an attempt at independence had been crushed by the Russian Czar. He hoped to reach Europe by way of the rugged and unexplored North American wilderness, possibly by contacting the fur traders of Hudson's Bay Company.

II. To get to Alaska he had to fight his way across Siberia and join fur thieves who were looting the Indians. Subienkow was attempting to learn geography from the natives, hoping to eventually escape to a more civilized area.

III.    A new leader arose, Malakoff, who lead the band of fur thieves deeper into the wilderness, eventually forcing the Indians into slave labor to build a fort. The Indians who tried to escape were brutally punished.

IV.    The women and children were held captive, forcing the Indians to hunt and trap fur for the thieves. But the Indians revolted, burning the fort and killing the surviving fur thieves by slowly torturing them to death.

V.    Subienkow has to watch as they kill Big Ivan. He is being held to the last since he lashed the face of Yakaga. Subienkow does not mind dying, but he hates the thought that the Indians will reduce him to a whimpering pile of flesh.

VI.    Subienkow tells Makamuk, the chief, that he will not die because he has a powerful medicine that will prevent them from killing him. He asks the chief what he would give to learn the medicine's secret.

VII.    Makamuk says he will give him his life and make him a slave the rest of his life. Subienkow is scornful. The chief then says he would not make him a slave, but Subienkow asked for more than that.

VIII. Subienkow demands that he receive a sled, dogs, and six warriors to provide him safety on his return to the base camp called Michaelovski Redoubt.

IX. Makamuk notices a scar on Subienkow's neck and says that the medicine is weak. Subienkow replies that it was a very strong person, stronger than Big Ivan, who drove that stroke, and that the medicine was weak because he lacked enough special berries at the place where the wound was made, but that there are plenty of these berries around their camp.

X. Makamuk agrees to provide the sled, dogs, and warriors, but Subienkow sneers that he was too slow in granting his demands, and that he now wants one hundred beaver, one hundred pounds of fish to feed the dogs, two sleds to carry the furs, and his rifle returned.

XI. Yakaga asks how they would know that the medicine is real. Subienkow explains that he will go into the woods (accompanied by twenty warriors) and pick the ingredients, then when ready he will smear it on his neck and the strongest of the Indians can take an ax and strike his neck three times.

XII. Makamuk agrees, but Subienkow says he answered too slowly, and now he demands more, he wants Makamuk's daughter. Makamuk agrees, but says that he personally will get to use the ax. Subienkow, with ill-concealed anxiety, makes the point that he must be allowed to apply more of the medicine to his neck between each of the blows.

XIII. Yakaga and the chief decide that they will kill Subienkow when they learn the secret of his medicine as he will not cover his whole body, or if he does, they will be able to kill through an uncovered spot.

XIV. Subienkow quickly picks the ingredients. Makamuk and Yakaga watch as he mixes them together. He also needs the finger from a man and wants to cut off Yakaga's finger. (Just a small finger, he says, when Yakaga put his hands behind his back and scowled.)

XV. Makamuk commands Yakaga to give him a finger but Yakaga points to all of their dead bodies lying around. Subienkow says that it must come from a live person, so Yakaga cuts a finger from Big Ivan, who is still barely alive, and tosses it to Subienkow.

XVI. He rubs the medicine on his neck. When Big Ivan regains consciousness and starts flailing around in the snow, Subienkow demands that they kill Big Ivan to stop the noise. He makes Makamuk show that he can use the ax like a man, then places his head on the block.

XVII. Makamuk strikes a hard blow, cutting off Subienkow's head—and then realizes that he has been fooled. Subienkow had escaped their torture, and the chief was laughed at. He lost his position as chief and would forever be known as "Lost Face."

# PREDATOR OF SOULS

by Scott E. Power

*This tale by Scott Power is a morality tale, which brings to mind the ancient morality tales that a medieval wandering minstrel or story teller would concoct. It's an entertaining story that deals with betrayal of trust and what happens to someone who is disposed to evil in the face of a great and good man.*

**M**any years ago in 1598, when the North American wilderness belonged to its rightful owners, there was a Cree shaman named Eagle Eyes, who was very wise and very old. He was called Eagle Eyes because he could see into the future.

Eagle Eyes was a holy man in his tribe. Tribe members honored him and followed his sage advice. He had been the spiritual leader of his tribe since the age of ten—a sacred number within the Cree culture— when the tribe became convinced of his supernatural aptitude. The young boy had walked up to a wild timber wolf and touched its head, caressing the wolf's fur. The wolf stood still, immediately sitting at rest in a submissive manor, showing all the witnesses that this little boy had supernatural power: the power to command wild animals into submission.

Later that day the little boy predicted a "ground storm" that would destroy the plains by "swallowing the grass." Two days later an earthquake hit north of the tribe's camp and 25 acres of the earth's surface sank into itself. It was on this day the tribe named the little boy Eagle Eyes, appointing him the spiritual leader and shaman of the tribe.

One day many years later, a woman in the tribe was in labor, giving birth. She was having extreme difficulty, so Eagle Eyes assisted in the birth. It was a very scary time. The woman was in great pain and near death. However the shaman was able prevent a tragedy by delivering the baby without harm to the mother. It was a boy. And something unusual happened when the baby was born: It did not cry. Because he sensed that something was wrong, Eagle Eyes spanked the baby to provoke it, but it did not work. Eagle Eyes looked into the baby's eyes and saw that it was alive and well. Immediately the mother named the baby boy Wacha, Cree for Strong Spirit.

As Wacha grew up, Eagle Eyes sensed there was something very special about the boy. As he talked with the boy, he realized that Wacha was an old soul, probably in his fourth incarnation. He was wise beyond his years and very interested in things unseen, spiritual matters, and shamanic powers. Eagle Eyes began to teach Wacha the ways of the shaman, making him an apprentice.

As Wacha grew older, he became very confident in his abilities and spiritual knowledge. Eagle Eyes had taught him well. Something began to stir within Wacha, something powerful. Wacha started to become aware of himself. He became conscious of his spiritual power. He desired more. And he wanted more knowledge. Curiosity grew within him. At night while the rest of the tribe was sleeping, Wacha would meditate, searching his soul for answers he did not have.

One day, Wacha asked Eagle Eyes about his thirst for the unknown. Immediately the wise shaman explained the danger of searching for such answers:

"There is only confusion in knowledge. Trust only in the Great Spirit. Trust not what you think. Trusting the mind over the Spirit is certain death. Trust in the Spirit and there is life forever. The Spirit never dies. Mind and its knowledge die and are gone forever. Trust not the tricks that the mind plays on the body. Mediate on what the Great Spirit has shown us, not on the Unknown. To do otherwise is certain death."

This upset Wacha greatly. He left Eagle Eyes's tepee feeling very angry, disappointed in what his mentor had said. Wacha didn't understand. He didn't think it was fair. He wanted more than what he had. More knowledge, more spiritual power. No! For Wacha this advice would not do. He would take it upon himself to probe even harder for the Unknown, for the answers he sought. He would continue his nightly mediations despite what Eagle Eyes had told him.

As time passed and Wacha continued to search the Unknown, something in him began to change. His demeanor and his posture changed. He became very sour faced and slouched over. He began to take on the appearance of an older person, one up in the seasons. Wacha's attitude changed, too. He become more withdrawn. He stopped speaking to others. He stopped smiling. And he started to hate Eagle Eyes.

Wacha became bitter about what his mentor had taught him. He felt that Eagle Eyes had cheated him out of vital knowledge about the Unknown. Wacha hated Eagle Eyes passionately. So, he devised a plan. He would cast a spell to steal Eagle Eyes's spirit from his body and be rid of him for good!

So, using his spiritual powers, Wacha cast a spell. He called for a wolf to wander into camp and brush against Eagle Eyes's leg and steal his spirit on contact.

Wacha couldn't wait for his spell to take hold. He began to fantasize about how great life would be without Eagle Eyes. Now Wacha would become the tribe's new shaman!

Later that day Eagle Eyes was found dead, lying in his tepee. There was no sign of physical harm being done, but his body was lifeless on the floor.

When questioned, the tribe member who found the body said he saw a timber wolf leaving Eagle Eyes's tepee, which is what caused him to peer inside. Wacha listened carefully, trying to appear concerned. All the while he was laughing on the inside;

a very evil spirit began to be grow inside Wacha. Others from the tribe, not knowing what was really going on, approached Wacha about becoming shaman immediately. He accepted.

It was a very dangerous time in the life of the tribe.

Early the next morning another wolf was spotted, this time leaving Wacha's tepee. Soon after Wacha's body was found dead on the floor. As people gathered in and around Wacha's tent to examine his body and mourn this double tragedy, Eagle Eyes walked through the crowd. People began to faint, falling to the ground. They thought they were seeing a dead man walking. Quite the contrary, Eagle Eyes was alive!

Once the tribe knew that it was truly him and not some ghostly illusion, Eagle Eyes explained that Wacha had cast a spell for a wolf to steal his spirit, which indeed worked and was why his body laid dead. But what Wacha didn't realize was that Eagle Eyes's power over animals would remain intact, and that he could control the wolf's actions.

So during the early morning Eagle Eyes—his spirit still with the wolf—went into Wacha's tepee and pulled Wacha's spirit out of his body and into the wolf. Then he went back to his own tent and rubbed up against his day old corpse, swapping his spirit back. He then condemned Wacha to a life trapped inside an animal's body, never to be reversed.

# STORY OUTLINE

I.    A Cree Indian boy became the tribe shaman by showing his control over a wolf and predicting a "ground storm" (earthquake).

II.   Many years later a boy was born who didn't cry at birth.

III.  This boy was called Wacha (Strong Spirit).

IV.   Wacha was not content learning the ways of the Great Spirit—he wanted to control it.

V.    He was counseled by Eagle Eyes to do otherwise, so he plotted revenge.

VI.   He caused a wolf to steal Eagle Eyes's soul one night and then assumed the role of tribal shaman.

VII.  But Eagle Eyes's soul caused the wolf to steal and trap Wacha's soul instead and to release his.

VIII. The tribe was rid of the evil spirit, and Eagle Eyes resumed his role as the tribal shaman.

# THE BOG

by William Forgey

*This original story went through a metamorphosis from its first telling which had the four friends canoeing into a hidden valley that was reached through a cave entrance. Originally called "The Hidden Valley," it did not explain how such a neat valley could remain unfound on the maps. So I invented the bog.*

Four members of Bensenville Troop 752 had been friends all of their lives. Scouting had allowed them to cement that friendship even further on many canoeing and camping trips near their home town and on several high adventure trips in Minnesota and New Mexico. But what lay ahead of them was far more sinister than any adventure they could have dreamed of . . . and it was going to happen practically in their own backyard.

Just outside of Bensenville there was a fairly large swamp, known locally simply as "The Bog." It was large enough to be deep and dense, but not large enough to attract attention of developers, park service personnel, or even conservationists. The bog had always been there. No roads went near it, no communities were positioned nearby—the bog sat by itself, tucked in a little-used portion of the state where time had passed it by.

The stagnant water in the bog seemed lifeless. It attracted no fishermen. There was an unusual scarcity of bird life, so no bird-watcher ventured into the hordes of mosquitoes to visit its remote water. Yet the bog seemed so dense that it was hard to imagine that there was not some living thing, even a whole slough of living things, within its borders.

Do not let me give the impression that this swamp was actually lifeless. Everyone who had ventured into the waters near its edge could vouch for the fact that indeed there was life in the swamp. The mosquitoes had neighbors—biting gnats, blackflies, swarms of bees, and although the waters seemed to produce few fish, leeches abounded.

Oh, the waters of the bog had been tested to determine if there were pollutants, radioactivity, or unusual chemicals dissolved in them. The tests had always shown nothing of interest. And so the bog continued to be abandoned.

It was abandoned for another reason beyond lack of interest: There just seemed to be something mysterious about its uncharted waters, perhaps something that might even be considered sinister. People tended to shy away from encountering the place—after all there was never a really good reason to go there anyway. Even the Indians who used to roam that area had apparently avoided the bog's confines.

But for Ralph, Bobby, David, and Chris, the bog held a special attraction. At first they paid little attention to it. They were having plenty of fun with Troop 752 just starting their camping adventures. Then those high adventure trips consumed their interest. But with these trips behind them, their thoughts turned to "The Bog." They knew how to handle the bugs they thought. They certainly knew how to camp and canoe. The swampy ground might make pitching a tent difficult—and perhaps there would be snakes and other creatures slithering along the ground—so they decided to pack along army surplus jungle hammocks with netting, besides their two tents.

As Ralph and Bobby were slightly older than the other two, they would each take the stern of a canoe, with David and Chris manning the bow. Water filtration pumps, fire starter, hand axe and saw, as well as sleeping bags and other gear were divided equally between the two canoes—in case something happened to one of them. Each boy carried a compass. There was a topographical map of the area, but it was featureless in the vicinity of the bog, except for map symbols representing a swamp.

The boys decided that they would leave the week that school was out for summer vacation. All was ready when the time came, and early one morning the four excited friends shoved off from the local highway bridge that spanned a watery section of the bog.

The wilderness opened up on all sides of them, with the air feeling heavy and smelling from the lush vegetation. They had expected mosquitoes so they were ready with the bug dope to keep them off. What they did not expect was the maze of islands, which they were finding difficult to navigate around. Frequently the channels were choked with weeds or simply played out, ending on a marshy shore.

Bubbles of marsh gas occasionally caused a sudden splash in the water near them, which seemed to accent the eerie feeling that they were all experiencing. The boys stopped on a marshy piece of land for lunch the first day, carefully purifying their water, which they acquired by shoving down on mats of floating seaweed and thus allowing water to percolate into the depression that formed. The canoes were sluggish in their forward motion because of the drag of seaweed, which also increased difficulty in paddling.

The weather favored them the first night so that by sunset they had selected a suitable campsite, unloaded the canoes, pitched the tents, and collected and sawed a store of firewood. It was easier to prepare drinking water this time, as there was a deeper channel by the island that they had chosen for the night. They were all prepared for bad weather. The boys cooked a good supper and, as the mosquitoes were not all that bad, they sat around the campfire—happy to be in the great outdoors, and on an adventure in an uncharted wilderness at that!

The strangest thing about that night was the almost total lack of wildlife. It was as if they were canoeing back into time, into some primitive swamp of the past. The deep stillness made many of the sounds around them seem amplified, and the boys' feeling a little keyed up also added to the startle each of them felt when they heard a "plop" in the water right next to their camp. No further swishing sounds were heard so the boys decided it was a lump of earth from the bank caving into the water.

In the night as they lay in their tents; once again they heard the swish of water.

It was barely 5:00 A.M. when daylight glowed along the eastern horizon of the bog. The two tents were capped and wreathed with smoky trails of fast melting mist. In the open spaces the ground was drenched with dew. Ralph lit the fire so that an hour later when the others got up, hot water would be ready and a bed of coals formed to make cooking breakfast less of a chore. He set forth on an exploration of his island but had gone barely 10 yards when alongside the bank a giant "whoosh" occurred. Ralph caught his breath at the sound, but then he soon saw what was happening. A large bubble of methane gas had escaped from the swampy floor of the bog, and it suddenly surfaced, bringing large chunks of rotten vegetation with it. A whole mat of this material floated and bobbed in the wake of the sudden gas escape.

Ralph cut his exploration of the island short and returned to the campsite. He had to wait patiently for about half an hour before the other boys got up, so he busied himself by fixing breakfast over the hot bed of coals that he had made, even though it was David's turn to be chef that day. After breakfast he told them of his discovery, about the source of the "swoosh" sound that they had heard the night before.

"Well that explains these clumps of floating debris that I've been having to push out of the way of the canoe," Chris remarked.

"Yeah, and some of those clumps are so big that they seem to be pushing right back," David, the other bowman, added.

"I've heard of something like this before," Bobby mentioned. "In one of the large swamps down south, maybe it was the Everglades or the Okeefenokee, bubbles of methane gas bubble up large amounts of debris from the swamp floor. Those mats float around and act as a platform for larger plants to live on. They become floating islands. When roots from the plants became long enough, they anchor the floating islands, which become permanently fixed in one place."

Finished with breakfast, the boys were anxious to shove off before the day became too warm. The reflection of the sun on the water and the stifling thickness of the air made the work of paddling their canoes all the more difficult.

"Ralph, what will we do if these islands we are charting float around and change their positions?" Bobby called over from his canoe. "We could get stuck back in this swamp forever!"

Ralph shouted back, "I've been thinking along those lines myself."

A fairly large stretch of open water promised to be a pleasant interlude from dragging their boats through weeds and trying to pole through the muck at the bottom. As they approached the open water, they noticed that the bottom deepened, deepened beyond the reach of their paddles.

But it was not to be an easy crossing. As the boys paddled, they suddenly realized that they were not making much progress toward the opposite shore. It seemed as if they were glued to the water's surface. The light breeze was not hurting or helping them. It caused a small chop of waves, which was insignificant. It just seemed as if they struggled without progress. The breeze calmed down the insect problem, and it gave the boys a chance to yank off their shirts and the insect head nets. Ralph soon realized that they were all sweating hard with everyone paddling furiously, almost savagely along, but they were getting nowhere.

"Rats," he shouted. "Hey, let's all cool it for a while. We're not going anywhere. Let's stop for a while and see what happens."

He got no argument from the others. They stopped and rested their paddles across the canoe gunnels, stretched their aching muscles, and wiped the sweat off their faces. They grinned at each other at first, feeling good about the workout they'd just had. Feeling weary, yet so strangely excited . . . . It was in the middle of that lake in the bewildering chatter and confusion of explanations, that, very silently, the ghost of something horrible slipped in and stood among them. It made all of their explanations seem childish and untrue. They exchanged quick, anxious glances—glances that were questioning, and expressive of the dismay that they were beginning to acknowledge. There was a sense of wonder, of poignant distress, of trepidation. Alarm stood waiting at their elbows. This ghost was a realization that something they did not understand was having its way with them.

They now rested quietly after their initial joyful excitement, feeling the little quivers that the light, choppy waves made against their canoes. But as they bobbed, their quietness was a manifestation of the fear that each of them was beginning to know. And none of them seemed to want to hear the others acknowledge this same fear. But something really did seem to have them in its grasp! It soon was becoming evident that their canoes were drifting toward the north side of the lake, almost at right angles to their original line of travel.

"Hey, if this lake wants us to go to that northern shore— well, let's just help it out a little. Let's start paddling!" With that almost cheerful statement from Ralph, everyone bent to the task of paddling out of this lake, which they were beginning to fear. Even then it seemed as if their progress just was not what it should be, that the lake held them with some invisible glue.

Even with this slow progress, the marshy shore of the north end soon came close enough to view easily from the canoes.

"Check it out," Chris remarked.

The shore seemed to be penetrated at regular intervals by streams that were flowing away from the lake. The land between these streams was marshy, so swampy that no obvious stopping place was evident.

"Our next campsite will be knee deep in water if something better doesn't appear," Chris continued.

Small, swampy islands located along the north shore were similarly unsuitable for camping.

"We've got to find someplace not only dry enough, but where we can find firewood, or we'll be stuck with just our gas stove. I'd rather be able to build a fire around this spooky place," commented Bob.

There was ready agreement on that, so that even though the boys were capable of pitching hammocks above the swampy ground and cooking with their Peak 1 stoves, they anxiously sought a piece of real estate where they could construct a more secure campsite.

After several hours of probing the streams, searching amongst the islands, and drifting along the shore, the boys found what appeared to be an almost ideal site.

"Jeez," this place looks like it was constructed for a campsite. This may not turn out so bad after all," one of them blurted out enthusiastically as they unloaded the canoes and started squaring away their gear.

There was a restless feeling in camp that evening, and none of the boys wanted to leave the protection of the campfire. It was as if something was alive out there, something moving—slowly, almost unperceived—but yet most assuredly moving about them. The very land seemed alive. The boys felt as if there were other people out there with them.

That night they were sure of it.

The swirling and sucking sound of the water washing along the shore, as well as the feeling of dread that they all seemed to have, caused the boys to gather as much firewood as possible and maintain their fire late into the night. The eerie night noises prompted them to peer out now and again into the black void of the night. Suddenly Chris saw something! It was a campfire flickering on an island about a mile away. Someone must be there! They all looked and watched as the small campfire burned down too low for them to see any more. After it disappeared, they all watched carefully for some sign of life, but they neither saw nor heard anything the rest of the night.

The mystery of that night deepened the next day when they decided to leave their camp set up but canoe over to the island where they thought they had seen the fire. There was a long, oval-shaped island, with large bushes in the center and several clearings, but no evidence of a fire. They spent the day searching other likely spots, but they could not find any evidence of the people whose fire they saw the night before.

The next night they again kept vigil by the fire. Sure enough, at about the witching hour of midnight, they again saw the fire flicker into life. As they watched, they thought they could see people moving around the fire. It was just too far away to tell for sure. Although there was surely more of the bog to explore, this seemed to be the crux of the mystery—to find out if a lost race of people were living back here.

The next day they again canoed over to the island where they had seen the campfire. They still could see no evidence of the campsite or indication of where the fire might have been built. Christopher designed a plan to solve the mystery. He decided that it would be a good idea for them to move the island and camp out there instead of staying where they were. But their present spot was so ideal that the others would not agree. They would have to cut firewood and canoe it over to the new site, the island seemed too damp, the clearings were small, and the bushes probably had too many mosquitoes. They all had reasons why they would not camp there, all that is except Christopher. When he could not get the others to agree to spend the night there, Christopher announced he would do it himself.

"You've got to be crazy, Chris," Bobby, his canoeing partner, told him. But Christopher was determined to solve the mystery.

"And besides you guys, the camp is only about a mile away. We can shout back and forth if we need to. I'll keep my fire burning all night if I'm scared, and one of you do the same. It won't be that bad."

But the others were buying none of it. They did not want anything to do with the swampy, mysterious island. They spent the rest of the day breaking out Christopher's camping gear from the rest of theirs and gathering the firewood, food, and purified water that he would need. By nightfall they had him in his camp, and they were back at theirs. As darkness fell, the fires burned brightly in both camps.

Occasionally the boys shouted across the water to each other. Chris's voice sounding so alone and far away. At just about midnight, Bobby was poking the fire with a stick, watching the sparks leap skyward. He looked up just in time to see Chris's campfire suddenly disappear! He thought, "Boy, is he a brave one. I'd probably keep my fire going all night."

Thinking to reassure Chris a little, he called over, "Hey, Chris! Did the boogy man get you?"

But there was no reply. Bobby shouted several more times, with the other guys also joining in. But they were to receive no answer from Chris's camp that night.

At first light the next day, the three anxious boys hopped into the canoe and paddled over to Chris's campsite. His canoe was floating free, not nestled up against the shoreline where Chris's camp should have been. When I say "should have been," I mean precisely that. The boys felt a sense of panic and sickness in the pits of their stomachs when they could find no trace of Chris's camp whatsoever.

"It's just like the fires we have been seeing the previous two nights," David remarked. "There is not a sign anyone has ever been here since the beginning of time."

The boys widened their search, checking nearby islands and the shoreline, but they could find no trace of Christopher. Because they had his canoe, they knew that he did not canoe away. Their great adventure had suddenly turned into a horrible nightmare.

Late in the afternoon, after checking all of the surrounding areas several times, even desperately calling his name during moments of panic and anger, the boys returned with the two canoes to their campsite.

They sat around their camp in a state of shock and disbelief, discussing what they should do. They felt the overwhelming urge to travel back to town and request help. But they did not want to leave Christopher by himself, wherever he was. There was a remote chance that they could still solve the mystery of the island.

Before dark Bobby came to a decision. He announced to the other guys that he was going to spend the night at Chris's island to see if he could solve the mystery. Ralph and David objected, but Bobby would not give in.

"I owe it to Chris to see if I can find out what happened to him."

Bobby packed up his gear, taking his sleeping bag, his clothes, and materials for starting a fire. He took his canoe and paddled over to the island as the others watched. Both camps started a fire just before dark. That night a thin layer of fog caused the fire from Bobby's camp to glow peculiarly in the distance. Neither Ralph nor David were about to try to sleep. They watched Bobby's camp intently as the night wore on. They called back and forth, but the distance was too great to clearly hear what was being said. Then about midnight, the very thing that Ralph and David were dreading happened again. The light from the other camp suddenly went out! They were almost in a panic, but they could do nothing about it. They knew that canoeing in the pitch black would be hazardous. And they were too scared to consider leaving their camp. They could feel the blackness of the night crawl closer around them. The water gurgled and swished at the shoreline. The chill of the night and the surrounding dampness made the night unbearable.

The first crack of dawn found them madly paddling their canoe over to Bobby's island. But his campsite was not to be found! There was no evidence of fire, and there was no sign of Bobby's clothing, sleeping bag, or footprints. Nothing showing human habitation was left on the island.

The boys stood on the swampy island in a state of shock. They hardly knew what to do. Ralph wanted to go home, but David knew that he had to find the answer to this mystery and was not about to leave his friends behind. He would not listen to Ralph's pleas that they get out of there as fast as they could paddle. David sighted a gleam in the water that turned out to be Chris's and Bobby's canoe floating full of water. Both life jackets and one paddle were missing.

Back at their campsite Ralph and David talked it over. "How can we possibly go back now? We may never find this place exactly again. You know how these islands seem to be floating around. We may never come to this exact point on the lakeshore or find the island that Chris and Bobby were camping on? And how about the mysterious campfires that we saw before they disappeared? If someone is out here, we must make contact with them. We can't tell their parents that we left them behind." And with that David completed their discussion. Except for one more thing.

"Ralph, I know of only one way to solve this problem. We have to camp out on the island ourselves."

Ralph would hear none of it. He was not about to stay on

that island. "Well Ralph," David said. I'm going to take that canoe and go over there myself, tonight. I'm going to find out for myself what's going on."

Ralph could not believe his ears. He was not about to spend the night on that island. The campsite that they had was spooky enough. And now he would have to be there alone. But he was not going to the island!

They spent that day in brooding silence. Ralph was too mad at David to really talk to him much. That night David departed and set up his camp at the island. The night seemed to fall all too quickly for Ralph, and he was glad he had a good fire to hold back the edge of darkness that surrounded his camp. There in the distance was the flicker of David's campfire.

Then, almost precisely at midnight, the very thing that Ralph was dreading the most happened. The small flickering fire on the island disappeared. Ralph's heart was in his throat it seemed. He felt a sense of panic, for he knew that he was in this swamp all alone. But more than that, he felt an incredible lonesomeness. The best friends that he had in the world were no longer with him. And there was not a thing that he could do about it.

With daybreak Ralph canoed the lonely stretch to the island. Again he found nothing. He looked carefully to see if he was on the right island. Somehow it did not look quite right. He had tramped over the marshy area so much that he had begun to know it. Or so he thought. It's oblong shape seemed smaller to him. But there was no other island close enough that he could be mistaken about the location. It had been in sight from the campsite, and he had followed the same azimuth to reach it—a straight shot from the camp.

Ralph knew that he could really do nothing for his friends, but he was also worried about how to get out of this mess himself. It should not be all that hard to do, but this time he would have to do it alone. Still he could not tear down his camp and leave just yet. He would spend one more night at their campsite, still hoping that he might be able to make some sense of their disappearance.

That night he watched over the dark lake, with both fear and sadness as competing emotions. As he sat contemplating the events of the last several days, Ralph was suddenly jarred into action by what he saw in the distance. A flicker of light appeared from the island campsite! He yelled out as loud as he could, but each time he listened afterward, he heard only the swish of water in return. Soon the light again disappeared, but Ralph felt a sense of hope.

In the daylight his position did not seem so bleak. And as he gained his courage, he also resolved to do the very thing that he knew all along deep down inside of himself that he had to do. He would have to move his camp to that dreaded island. He would have to find out what the mystery of that place was for himself. He would not leave his friends behind, no matter what their fate—or no matter what his might become.

He broke camp early that afternoon and returned to the island. The ground in the middle of the island was spongy, but he was able to clear an area for a safe fire. He erected his tent. "Standing around here is like standing on a waterbed," he thought to himself, as he squared his campsite away. It was sure a let down from the comfortable camp where he had spent most of the previous week.

The wetness of the place made the camp miserable. Ralph decided to place his bedding and most of his gear in the canoe and tie the canoe to the shore, allowing it to float free. As darkness fell, he made sure that he had plenty of firewood on hand, some of which he had brought over from the other campsite. In fact he had about three times as much firewood as he thought he would need, certainly more than the others had brought.

With nightfall the dampness became even more noticeable. Hour, followed hour as Ralph stood around the eerie camp. Suddenly he heard a familiar sound, it was the swoosh of water as gas from the swamp's floor bubbled up to the surface. And although this attracted his attention, not too far away near the shore, he saw a flare of light upon the water's surface. He stared at it flickering, then climbed into his canoe for a better view, allowing the canoe to drift a little way from the island's edge. Suddenly there was a massive shift of the island, the entire center where his camp was located folding in on itself, his campfire disappearing in the rush of water and hiss of steam. A wave rocked his canoe as Ralph stared in disbelief. But he now learned the secret of the island.

The campfires that they had been seeing were actually will-o'-the-wisp, the phosphorescent light sometimes seen in the air over marshy places. And the island was a floating island, just as they had all known. But what they did not real-ize was that this floating island was not able to support their weight for a long period of time. The center of the island would suddenly sink under the weight of the campers stand-ing on it, just folding together and dragging the struggling vic-tims underwater. With each collapse the island had been growing smaller. And Ralph realized that his companions would be buried forever beneath the muck, quicksand, and water of the lake.

# STORY OUTLINE

I.     Four members of Bensenville Troop 752 had been friends all of their lives and they were looking forward to further high adventures in the mysterious bog that lay outside of town.

II.    Ralph, Bobby, David, and Chris left the week school was out to explore the bog by canoe.

III.   The found the marsh a strange place, with bubbles of marsh grass and mats of floating vegetation. The water and weeds seemed to slow their progress.

IV.    As they camped the first night, they heard strange plopping and swirling sounds in the water. Ralph later sees a large bubble of marsh gas come to the surface, thus explaining the sounds of the night.

V.     They enter a large stretch of open water but still find the paddling difficult. Drifting, they find that they are drawn to the north shore of the lake, where they find a good, dry campsite after much searching.

VI.    That night they built a large fire to ward off their fears. During the night Chris saw another campfire in the distance.

VII.    The boys search for the fire the next day, but they do not find it. The next night they again spot the fire. Chris decides to spend the night on an island where they think the fire may be coming from to investigate the mystery.

VIII.   The boys watch Chris's campfire that night, when suddenly it goes out. They shout over to him but receive no reply.

IX.     The next day they canoe to his island at daybreak but can find no trace of his camp. The canoe is found floating nearby. They search everywhere for Chris but cannot find him.

X.      Against the other boys' advice, Bobby decides he will also camp out on the island. They watch his campfire that night through a thin layer of fog, until it also suddenly goes out at about midnight.

XI.     The next day Ralph and David canoe over at daybreak, but again there is no trace of the campsite on the island.

XII.    David realizes that they cannot go back without solving the mystery. He ignores Ralph's pleas to leave and prepares to spend the night on the island.

XIII.   Ralph watches intently that night, when almost precisely at midnight David's flickering fire disappears.

XIV.  Ralph finds no trace of David or his canoe the next day. He spends the day searching and decides to spend one more night at the camp, hoping to learn something about their disappearances.

XV.  That night as he watched over the dark lake, he saw a flicker of light from an island campfire appear again. No one answers his shouts.

XVI.  He broke camp the next day determined to solve the mystery of the island by himself.

XVII.  He moves extra firewood to the boggy island and makes his camp. He leaves his canoe floating but tied to the shore.

XVIII.  During the night he suddenly sees a fire nearby. He gets into his canoe to view it better and realizes that they have been looking at a methane swamp gas flare, a will-o-the-wisp.

XIX.  As he watches the flare, the island collapses, folding in the middle from the weight of the firewood. He realizes that his friends, standing in the camp in the middle of the floating island, made it collapse, causing them to be sucked into the muck, quicksand, and water below.

# THE WALKING STICK

by William Forgey

*Have you ever had one of those days, especially when you are hiking or climbing, when you just do not have the zip and vigor that everyone else has? On one such an occasion, I decided that perhaps I was just contending with an evil spell, for I certainly could not be that much older or in that much worse shape than the rest of my party. That got me started thinking about a possible source of an evil spell for a nephew who just could not leave his uncle's things alone.*

Mike had a walking stick that used to be his uncle's. He always wanted to take it camping. Hiking with it now, with the rest of the kids envious of his stick, was something he was enjoying, sort of. Sort of? Well, Mike couldn't really enjoy this moment as much as he wished. You see, the stick didn't belong to him . . . yet. It was still his uncle's, and he had been warned to leave it alone. But there it was in his grandpa's house, down in a closet filled with things—all still owned by his uncle.

But that stick. It was special and stood out from the rest of the items—even his uncle's military uniform, the one with the medals. You see his uncle had always made it clear to Mike to stay away from that stick. He wasn't to touch it, play with it, even take it out of the closet—and here he was taking it on a camping trip with the other boys in the scout troop, just as if it were his.

He never understood why he wasn't to play with it. His uncle had never told him. In fact he had always scolded Mike for coming near it or for even asking questions about it. His uncle had been in Vietnam for many years, and there were many things that he said that Mike knew he would never understand fully. This stick was obviously part of the stuff he had brought home from that war. Mike felt hat there was something sinister about it, something evil. It didn't look like much. Just a stiff, light and straight pole. But the color was black. It came to a sharp point and broadened as it went up to the top, where it formed a smooth, flat head.

The stick would have been just right for his uncle to use

as a walking stick, but it was a little tall for Mike. Still, it fit well enough in his hand as they scrambled over the rough ground. Mike was always having to hurry a little to keep up with the bigger guys. The sun was becoming a little hot; the ground was uneven at times, with logs and stones covering the trail here and there; and now insects were becoming both-ersome—especially in this heat. It seemed that the insects were bothering him more than the other guys. Maybe he was sweating more. As he looked at the boy ahead of him, he could tell that Jim looked comfortable. His friend was walking along the trail in an almost carefree manner. Jim had not soaked through his shirt, but Mike had. The heat was cloud-ing his vision, hurting his brain, even bothering his hearing.

The trip became even harder as the trail led up the hill to a fire tower. A natural spring had been tapped with a faucet, providing water for the little campground about 300 feet beneath the hilltop. As they reached the campsite, the other kids wanted to run on ahead to scramble up the tower. Mike was too exhausted to even consider climbing that last 300 feet of hill. He flopped to his back at the last remaining tent site, breathing heavily in the stifling hot air of that summer after-noon.

The sounds of the kids in his troop faded away, up the hill. The drone of the insects seemed louder and muffled the happy sounds coming from his friends. He swatted at them aimlessly, too tired to open his eyes. The hot sun made the vegetation smell musty and strong. The babble of voices seemed to continue in the background. As he lay exhausted against his pack, he hoped he would never have to move again. Clutching the walking stick, which he laid along his side, he became more aware of the strong smells of the forest.

Now he was even less aware of the incoherent chatter in the background, coming from the hill above him.

He paid no attention, that is, until suddenly it dawned on him that there was something different about those voices. He could not understand even an occasional word. The voices were making choppy, peculiar sounds. The insects were competing with their swarming and buzzing. Strange that his friends did not seem to notice this horrible weather, these horrible bugs. What were they doing anyway? He no longer heard the occasional sound of his scoutmaster's voice.

Mike lazily opened his eyes. What he saw shocked him wide awake. The trees had changed! The weeds, the bushes, the forest—it all had changed! Just the heat was there . . . and those mosquitoes. And the voices from above him on the hill.

But the voices were different. Mike wasn't sure what he noticed first: the fact that he could see no other camping gear around him, that he was in a thick jungle of vegetation, or that the voices he heard were not those of his friends!

His first impulse was to call out, to yell his head off for help! But there was something scary about those voices. They were excited, shouting to each other, crashing through the thick brush above him. He could tell that the people making the noises were thrashing the brush as they walked along through it, as if they were in a straight line beating the bushes, trying to flush something, or someone, out!

He thought that the voices were sinister, gruff. He realized that he should take no chances with these people. He must hide. He hated leaving his spot because he was afraid that he would only get helplessly lost. Yet he feared for his life.

Still clutching the walking stick, Mike slid down the hill under the cover of a layer of large leafed plants. The dirt from

**113**

the forest floor stuck to his sweaty legs and clothing, the stick was slick in his sweaty hands. His movement must have attracted attention on the hill above him for there was a commotion—the people all seemed to be coming, crashing down the hill directly toward him!

The jungle floor was steep, steep like the jungle-covered hills in Vietnam must have been where his uncle had served during the war. Mike was able to slide faster and faster, and he desperately tried to get away from the people streaming down the hill above him. As he looked up he could see them, coming closer and closer. He could make out the peculiar helmets, the red star on their helmets, their rifles.

The bushes whipped him as he slid down the hill toward a stream that he could hear below. The willow-like wands of brush were cutting at his face, arms, and legs. It didn't matter. Just as long as he could get away! A bush with bright orange flowers and long spike-like thorns struck him, leaving a large thorn stuck in his right arm.

Suddenly as he slid toward a large tree—CRACK! The walking stick slammed against the tree and was torn from his grasp! He suddenly plunged off a small gully, SPLASH into a stream of cold water!

With a shock he looked around. The forest was hardwood, he was not in the jungle anymore. The voices from above him were those of his friends, who were excitedly climbing down the hill after him, looking for him! Mike realized that the walking stick was not in his hands any longer. The weather was pleasant and cool. The bugs were gone.

Mike could never explain to his scoutmaster or his friends what had happened to him. And he could not find the walking stick, no matter how hard he looked. His mom took him to the doctor when he got home to have a large, strange thorn taken out of his arm.

But what was really strange was that his uncle was never seen or heard of again. All traces of him vanished—and Mike wondered if his uncle could have taken his place, deep in some mysterious jungle in Vietnam! He would never know.

# STORY OUTLINE

I.   Mike took his uncle's walking stick, a souvenir of the Vietnam War, with him on a hike with his scout troop—even though he had been warned to leave it alone.

II.  The troop was hiking in a forest up a hill to a fire tower.

III. While everyone else was enjoying the hike Mike felt hotter and hotter—and was bothered by the bugs.

IV.  When the troop reaches the campsite, he is too tired to scramble farther to the tower with the other kids. As he rests, he is surrounded by bugs and the heat.

V.   He becomes aware that the voices of his friends have changed; the vegetation has changed—he appears to be lost in a jungle.

VI.  He tries to get away from the people, probably Viet Cong, who are chasing him. As he crashes down hill toward a stream, he hits a tree and has the stick knocked away from him.

VII. After this crash, he realizes that he is back with his friends in a normal woods.

VIII. The stick is lost. His mother takes him to the doctor to have strange thorn removed from his arm. And his uncle disappears, never to be seen again.

# THE INDIAN HEAD

by Pat Sherwood

This original story by Pat Sherwood starts with a fabricated explanation of the source of the story, a technique used to establish credibility. The "credibility factor" has a profound impact in setting the proper mood, which increases the dramatic effect of a story.

Obviously his introduction should be changed to a more personalized and plausible source by the individual storyteller, unless the kids would feel that he or she also had camped in the high timber area of Washington State.

This story was passed on to me while on a camping trip high up in timberline in Washington State. An old-timer had wandered into our camp late one afternoon, and according the custom was asked to share our camp for dinner and a night's rest.

After supper we sat around the campfire finishing the last of the coffee. It was one of those cool, breezy evenings that always stays in your mind, dark, with just enough of a chill to turn up a collar and be thankful for the warmth and glow of the fire.

I remember looking across at the stranger who now shared our camp. He sat smoking a pipe, the whirls of smoke encircling his head, the light of the fire reflecting the whiteness of his beard, magnifying the lines that were cut deep into his face by constant exposure to the mountain winds. His eyes were clear and lively and seemed too young for the face they served. The old-timer's name has long since slipped from my memory, but I remember his face and the low, soft voice that spoke the slang of the woods well.

As the night grew darker, the conversation naturally turned to those things that go bump in the night. And on hearing that I was from Indiana, the stranger seemed to give an ear to some old voices in his memory. He then related this story, which has stayed in my mind for many years. As I sat there listening to his tale after a few moments, the past came to life again in the changing embers of the fire.

In the early 1820s, there was a small trading post nestled on a river bend in the southern part of Indiana, no more than

**119**

a three-day canoe north of Fort Vincennes. It has been said that George Rogers Clark may have passed through there on his way to defeat Hamilton at Vincennes.

The trading post was used by French trappers for many years before the revolution opened it up for the Americans. One of the Americans was a mountain of a man by the name of John Walker, "Big John" as the other trappers called him.

No one seemed to know just where John came from, and those that knew of him, knew better than to ask. It was said that he was as big as a tree, as broad and strong as any horse on the river, meaner than a badger, and as stubborn as they came. They said you had a better chance of convincing a mule he had his ears on backwards than to get Big John to change his mind or give in. About the only friend John had at the post was a fur buyer by the name of Austin Handley, and their friendship, at best, was limited to conversation over a shared bottle of whiskey.

John never stayed at the trading post long, preferring to be by himself and running his traps. When he was at the post, everyone gave him a lot of ground. Being simple of mind he'd cut your heart out for the fun of it. Even the Indians would give Big John a wide berth; they thought him crazy and bad medicine. But when it came to trapping furs, the other trappers all agreed, John was the best. He would stay out longer, trap the toughest of terrain, and when he did come to the trading post, he'd have the largest and most pelts of any trapper in the area.

This was the only thing that seemed important to John, finding the largest and best of pelts. He was always on the lookout for better areas to trap and bigger furs to take. Simple as he was one thing stayed ever in his mind, that the local

Indians always seemed to have larger and thicker furs than he did.

So Big John set out to find the elusive trapping ground that the local Indians kept so secret. His search took him all over the surrounding forest, through thick swamps, and over what seemed like every hollow in the territory. Finally John happened to stumble across a creek and decided to follow it upstream. He was completely unfamiliar with the area, so he made sure to mark his trail well. Eventually the creek took a wide turn, and just as he had hoped, the creek was run off from the largest beaver colony that John had ever seen.

The runways of the colony's hauling trails were well laid to grade and purpose. The runs were wide and big enough to send a canoe down. The freshly cut trees with their large teeth marks were enough to tell him that he was sitting in a trapper's paradise. No wonder the Indians kept this place so secret, the beaver there were as big as dogs and twice as fat.

But the beaver colony wasn't the only thing that John found that day. All about the area were totems and symbols of an Indian burial ground. John clearly understood that being there could only bring trouble. But if it was trouble those Indians wanted, they need go no farther, because John was not about to leave the trapping grounds that he had spent a lifetime trying to find.

The next few weeks were spent laying out traps and collecting the finest bundle of furs this side of the Canadian border. But winter was not far off, and soon he would have to prepare for his trip downstream to the trading post. John was sure the other trappers would be green as river moss when they laid their eyes on this set of furs. For the first time since John came to that region, he actually looked forward to going to the trading post.

But as it so often happens, John's jubilation was to be short lived. For one morning as John made his way up the creek to check his trapline, he found the trouble he knew would come. There in his path were two crossed war lances, the type common to the Indians of the area. He knew what the lances meant, the Indians were warning him not to go any farther. But they weren't going to scare John away from collecting the pelts that he worked so hard to get. So he went on to check the first of his traps. John didn't have to get very close before he knew there would be no beaver caught in this trap. Even from a distance he could see the Indian lance that stood erect where his trap should be, a further warning for him to stay away. Big John felt no fear, but rather he was enraged at the thought that the local natives would dare defile his traps.

John hurried along his route, checking each of his traps, only to find that each had been opened or broken, each with a lance stuck through the center. By the time he made it to the burial grounds where the last of his traps were placed and finding these also destroyed, John was crazy with anger. And when that anger had fully consumed him, he screamed out at the forest horizon, vowing to avenge the wrongs done to him. But no sooner had the words left his mouth, than his eyes looked up at the ridge that kept guard over the valley from the north. There, mounted on their war ponies, sat three young braves, their faces painted in bright colors, shields and lances at their sides. All was quiet except the faint echoes of John's vow fading in the distance. The eyes of the four men locked on one another.

Suddenly the raging anger that had consumed John's

mind, spilled forth in a floodlike stream of curses and vows of eternal vengeance. John raised his rifle above his head, shook it at them, and challenged the three warriors to come and meet his wrath.

His challenge was answered in a heartbeat. The brave on the chestnut pony raised his lance, let out a war whoop, and came charging down into the valley directly at John. As he raised his rifle, John almost had to smile at how simple it was going to be, and with a single shot, the young warrior died half way down the hill.

But no sooner had the shot rang out, than the brave atop a large gray pony let out a blood curdling scream and came charging into the valley. John had started to reload but soon realized there was not enough time, so he dropped his rifle and quickly pulled his pistol from his belt. By the time John turned to shoot, the brave was nearly on top of him, leaving no time to get off a good shot. The bullet struck the Indian in the midsection, knocking him from his mount, at the same time his lance cut into John's side, twisting him to the ground. John's wound was not severe, and luckily the lance did not stick. The warrior was quick to get up and came at John with knife in hand. But the young brave's wound slowed him down. It was John's knife that found its mark first, and the young brave fell dead.

John struggled to his feet, and his eyes turned toward the last of the three braves. Their eyes met, and even at that distance, John could tell that this warrior was different from the others. Although young, John could see that the brave had fought in many battles by the tokens that hung from his war lance. He was more experienced that the other two.

The brave seemed to wait for John to regain his balance

and prepare himself for the fight that was about to come. It was John who made the first move. He quickly reached for his rifle, hoping to be able to reload in time. The brave reacted quickly, and letting out a war whoop, he charged down the trail with his lance and shield at the ready. John worked feverishly to reload, but the charging warrior would not allow him enough time, for with a mighty heave, the Indian threw the lance, John made a quick move to his right, avoiding the lance by only inches. It stuck in the ground at the big man's feet. As John twisted around, he could see the warrior spin his pony about. The feathered warrior drew his tomahawk and prepared to make another charge. John reached out for the only weapon he had available, the Indian's own lance. He grabbed the lance firmly, set his feet, and waited for the brave to charge.

John's eyes were fixed and glowed with anger as the thundering pony closed down on him. John lashed out with the lance, only to have it glance off the young brave's shield. The warrior quickly turned his war pony and charged again. Again John lashed out with the lance, only this time it shattered as it struck the shield. The force threw John to the ground. John rolled, trying to get to his feet. He could hear the Indian's pony pulling up and turning for another pass. Seeing his rifle, John lunged for it, grabbed it on the roll, and somehow managed to get to his feet. Holding the rifle by the barrel, he waited for the next charge.

John's eyes were set with anger, his mind ablaze with hate! He cursed and challenged the brave to come at him again. The young warrior turned and pulled up his pony. Looking at the intruder, the Indian's eyes also filled with anger. Letting out a war whoop and kicking his pony, he charged again, his tomahawk at the ready. Just as the brave converged on him, John made a move to the right and swung the rifle with all his might, striking the Indian across the chest. The blow knocking the Indian from his mount and spun the big man to the ground.

John rolled, trying to get to his feet, his body not doing what his mind asked. He managed to get on his hands and knees and looked over to his foe. With a knife in hand, the young Indian warrior was also trying to regain his feet. He, too, was looking toward his foe. Slowly they rose to their feet and standing face to face knew this would be the final battle for one of them.

John was much larger than his foe, but the Indian was quicker. If John had fought anyone tougher in his life, he couldn't remember who it was. The battle seemed to go on forever. Both men were cut, bruised, bleeding, and near exhaustion. But the fight went on, neither giving ground to the other.

Finally the big man's strength won out, and John held the knife to the throat of the brave who had fought so hard. Without blinking so much as an eyelash, and with more strength than John knew he had left, he cut the Indian's throat so deeply that he severed the Indian's head from his body. John decided to keep the head as a totem.

After tending his wounds, John wrapped the head in a leather sack, gathered his gear, and slowly made his way back to his cabin. He was totally exhausted when he collapsed on his bed. His last thoughts as he drifted off were that he needed to get to the trading post and have his wounds tended to properly, that he would pack his furs and make the trip as soon as he awoke.

Sleep didn't bring the rest that John had hoped for. He

tossed and turned all night, sometimes hot, other times cold. At some time in the gray of the morning, that void between the end of night and the beginning of day, John half awoke. There next to him stood an Indian. He appeared to be a medicine man, shaking a rattle and chanting something that John couldn't understand. Everything seemed like a dream. John's mind was too exhausted to interpret what was going on; he passed back into the darkness of sleep.

John awoke with a startle, the events of the night before still fuzzy in his brain. As he tried to clear his mind, John made his way to the cabin door. A breath of fresh air might help clear his head. His body ached and his wounds hurt as he crossed the floor. The sunlight nearly blinded him as he opened the door.

But John wasn't ready for what awaited him outside. There on the porch of his cabin were the shattered lance and the shield of the slain warrior. Not ten paces away laid the headless body wrapped in a blanket and covered with beads and trinkets.

The shock of what he saw shook John's already confused mind. Almost as if in a trance, he slowly walked toward the body. He couldn't understand why the Indians would bring the remains here. They could have buried him where he fell in their burial grounds. As John drew closer, he became aware of a smell, noxious, like an unclean hide hung to dry in the sun.

Suddenly, almost as if a sixth sense warned him, John spun around. There, only a few steps from him stood the medicine man he had seen the previous night. Slowly, softly so John wouldn't miss a word, he spoke. John could understand most of what he said because he had had dealings with the Miami tribe, which lived in these parts. And although the language seemed the same, it was a different dialect.

It seemed that the young brave was the son of a tribal chief from the north, perhaps a cousin to the great warrior chief, Tecumseh. And befitting his position, he deserved a burial with many great gifts and tokens. But he needed to be buried whole, for without his head he would not be able to find his way to the next world. If John did not return his head willingly, the great warrior would wander forever between the two worlds. And many bad things would befall John the remainder of his days. With that the Indian was gone, leaving John standing trancelike in front of his cabin.

When he finally got a grip on himself, John turned to find that the body was also gone. Quickly he got back to the cabin, figuring that surely warriors would attack and take the head from him. And if they ever thought he would return that head of his own free will, they were sadly mistaken. Being as stubborn as he was, he figured that he'd give them a fight they'd never forget. John closed and barred all the windows and doors, took what little furnishing he had, and barricaded himself in.

Most of the day was spent with rifle in hand, with the head, still wrapped in the leather sack, next to him. Except for a few sudden outbursts of cussin' and swearin' John just sat there waiting for the Indians to return. Along about evening he built a fire, fixed himself something to eat, and again settled back and waited. He must have dozed off because all of a sudden he realized that the smell from the morning was back. Quickly he reached down and grabbed the sack next to him and threw it across the cabin. As it hit the floor, John heard the most gruesome moan he'd ever heard. It sent chills up his spine, and he moved away from the noise.

The moan came back, and as John looked in that direction,

he saw the ghostly figure of an Indian standing in the corner. Dressed in buckskin and beads, he held in one arm his war lance and shield. In the other he held a headdress common to those parts. But above that Indian's shoulders there was nothing. There before John stood the headless apparition of the warrior he had slain.

John's heart felt as if it would jump clean out of his chest. The moaning seemed to get louder as the ghost seemed to float, slowly toward John. He brought up his rifle and fired at the apparition, but the bullet went on through and struck the wall behind. John dropped the rifle and watched as the ghostly brave slowly raised his arms and cupped his hands in what appeared to be a pleading motion. John knew what the headless figure wanted. He had to force his body to move as he slowly crawled across the floor toward the sack he had thrown. Without taking his eyes off the spirit, he felt around until he found the sack and pulled it to his chest. As he did the moaning seemed to quiet a bit. John sat clutching the sack to his body, staring at the haunting figure before him.

Suddenly, as if he had gone completely mad, John started laughing, a wild hysterical laugh. He cursed and swore at the brave and told him that he would not return the head the ghost sought. And John dared the specter to do his worst, for as long as he had the head there was nothing that it could do to him.

Suddenly a banshee-like scream filled the room, the fire flared up and as chilling a wind as John had ever felt swirled about the cabin. Things flew about the room as if they had minds of their own. The scream and moans grew so load that it hurt the big man's ears. John curled up on the floor, tucking the sack under him. Then, just as suddenly, the place was quiet. John remained on the floor, never looking up until the first rays of sunlight found their way into the cabin.

Wasting no time, John packed his canoe and started down the river. He figured if he really pushed and stayed at it all day, he could make the trading post by late evening. With the leather sack tightly strapped to his side, John paddled all day, never letting up. A strong current got him to the post about an hour after dark.

He quickly made his way to the post. After downing several large swallows of whiskey, John asked where he could find Austin Handley, his one and only friend there.

John found his friend at a cabin on the north end of the post. Over the better part of a bottle of whiskey, John told Austin the entire story of the Indian head, even showing him the head he carried in the sack. Now there's little doubt that Austin thought him completely mad, but he gave John a blanket and told him he could rest in the storage room that adjoined the cabin. Exhaustion and the drink make it easy for the big man to sleep.

Nobody knows for sure exactly why he awoke; it may have been the noxious smell or the sudden coldness that jolted John out of his sleep that night. But awake he was, and there standing over him was the ghost that now haunted him. Gone were the lance and shield. Nor did the apparition carry the headdress he had the previous night. But there was something else that the specter held. John tried to focus his eyes as the ghostly brave raised it to view. A large round item dangled from the hand of the ghostly arm. John looked harder at the object, and finally as his eyes adjusted, he could see that it looked familiar. Then a wave of sudden shock swept over him, his stomach twisted into a knot, his mouth open for a scream that wouldn't come. John knew what the object was—it was the dismembered head of Austin Handley. John rolled and stumbled as he tried to get to his feet, his head spinning and his legs like rubber.

The big man finally made it to his feet. Wobbly and clutching the walls for support, he tried to find the door, the leather sack still handing from his shoulder. As John stepped through the door, the Indian specter was already there waiting, laughing and holding the ghostly head of his only friend. John moved to the bed, still clutching the walls for support. There lying on the bed was the headless body of his friend.

If Big John Walker had managed to keep his mind up to then, now he lost it. He ran screaming into the night, tearing through the brush, breaking his way through the branches like the madman most thought he was. He ran till his once powerful body would no longer do what his mind asked, and then he collapsed. There he laid, crying and still clutching the leather sack that carried his torment. Somehow he became aware of the faint sound of an Indian's rattle, the sound growing slowly closer, and John knew who was there. With a sudden calmness and sense of relief, he offered up the sack without even looking up. He felt it taken from his hand and heard the chanting of the medicine man. There he lay, first crying, then whimpering until unconsciousness took over his exhausted body.

When he awoke he was aware of a feeling of coldness—and the stench that had become all too familiar to him. He clutched at the now empty sack that had carried the Indian brave's head. As John opened his eyes, he saw the forest slowly revolving before him. And there on the ground was a body—a headless body. And John realized with a jolt that

IT WAS HIS OWN HEADLESS BODY. As John slowly turned his head he found himself staring directly into the grinning face of the dead warrior. With a banshee yell the warrior flung John's head high into the air. With that, darkness came to Big John. It was the last sight that he ever saw.

# STORY OUTLINE

I. Big John Walker was a trapper in the early 1820s in Indiana, living not far from Fort Vincennes.

II. John Walker was half crazy, but he was the best trapper in the area. He found the secret Indian trapping around, but it was also part of a sacred burial ground.

III. He ignores the Indians' warnings not to trap there and is angered when they destroy his traps.

IV. Three braves accept his challenge to fight. Big John defeats all three, shooting the first, wounding the second with his pistol and killing him after a fight, but only after he had also been wounded.

V. Big John and the third Indian have a long and hard fight. At the end John gets the upper hand and cuts the Indian's throat so deeply that he severs his head from his body. He decides to keep the head as a victory totem.

VI.     He treats his wounds, gathers his gear an furs, and returns to the cabin, planning to leave the trading post for proper care as soon as he can.

VII.     That night he tosses and turns in bed but is finally awakened by a medicine man shaking a rattle and chanting. John feels that he is in a dream and goes to the door for some fresh air.

VIII.     There on the porch of the cabin is the shattered lance and shield of the slain warrior, and not ten paces away his head-less body wrapped in a blanket and cov-ered with trinkets.

IX.     A stench hung in the air. John turned around and the medicine man was there, saying that the warrior needed to be given a funeral and that the head must be returned, or the brave would wander between this world and the next—and that a curse would be on John the rest of his days.

X.     When John recovered from his shock, he saw that the medicine man and the body were gone.

XI.     John stayed ready with his gun all day,

expecting the Indians to attack, but an attack never came. After he ate supper that night, the headless warrior appeared, amidst a stench and feeling of cold—pleading for his head.

XII.    John refuses the warrior's plea for his head—a banshee scream fills the air, the fire blazes, and then all is quiet.

XIII.    Early the next day, Big John packed up and headed for Fort Vincennes, taking the head with him.

XIV.    When he reached the trading post, John looked up his one and only friend, Austin Handley, and told him the entire story. Handley allows him to sleep in a spare room that night.

XV.    A cold feeling and the stench return that night, awakening Big John. When he opens his eyes, he sees that the headless brave's outstretched arm is holding the head of his friend Austin Handley.

XVI.    Big John stumbles into the next room, and there on the bed lies the headless body of his friend.

XVII.    John stumbles screaming from the cabin, carrying the leather sack with the Indian's head.

XVIII.  He collapsed in the woods, exhausted. When John awoke, he saw the forest revolving around him, then he recognized a headless body on the ground in front of him—IT WAS HIS OWN HEADLESS BODY!

XIX.  John slowly turned his head until he was facing the grinning face of the dead warrior. The warrior yelled a war cry and threw John's head high into the air.

XX.  Darkness then came to Big John—it was the last sight that he saw in his life.

# THE PLAID COFFIN

as told by William Forgey

*This is a traditional and famous folk tale, modified for campfire storytelling.*

This story took place a long time ago back in the late 1800s. In the western part of the county back in the foothills lived a family of four: mother, father, son and daughter. The daughter was beautiful. She was seventeen years old, her hair was long and golden yellow. Her cheeks always had a red flush to them, but she used nothing for color, except every now and then when she would go to a square dance, she might peach her cheeks just a little.

One May morning the young girl took ill. Her cheeks lost their rosy color and her skin, which used to be so clear, lost its glow and turned gray. The mother worked with the girl. She gathered herbs, boiled them into tea, and gave it to her. But the girl continued to get sicker. Her health was failing, and by the morning sun, the girl was gone.

Her spirit left her silently. Her mother was asleep in the early hours, and when she awoke, she saw the girl lying still on the bed. The mother rubbed her eyes to chase away the sleep. She tried to see if the girl was breathing, but she was not. The bed was quiet.

The mother went over and touched her daughter. She felt a chill—a cold, gray feeling from the child. The mother walked quietly over to the window and looked out. She stood there for several minutes, watching the fog spin off in patterns. Then the tears came. She could see nothing.

Later the father and the son took mattocks and shovels to the family graveyard and spent most of the day digging the grave. When they came back to the house, the mother was standing on the porch, and her eyes were pained with the tears of a day full of weeping.

"We should use the old cedar box," she said, and she went back into the house.

The father and the son climbed the loft of the barn, and they saw the cedarwood box. It was long and narrow. The father opened it. It was lined with cotton plaid, lined completely, underneath the lid, the sides, and on the bottom. It was complete with a feather mattress and a feather pillow.

The father stood on top of the loft and lowered the box while the son steadied it. Together they carried it to the house. When they arrived, the mother said, "She's ready."

The girl lay on the bed dressed in a white gown. "I put my wedding dress on her," said the mother. "She's just the same size as I was then."

The father and son took the box to the grave site, where they buried her. The father threw the last bit of dirt on the fresh mound. Then they returned to the house. The son was exhausted. He went upstairs and fell asleep.

Suddenly, in the middle of the night, he was awakened by a scream! AAAUUUGGGHHH! He didn't know where it came from. He looked about his room and out of the window, but there was no moon so he could see nothing. Then he thought of his sister. He heard another scream. It was fuller and louder and shattering, and he realized that it was coming from downstairs.

He quickly dressed. When he got down the stairs, he saw his father standing beside his mother. He had her hand in his. He was comforting her and trying to get her to lay back down. The mother screamed again. The boy felt chills shutter throughout his body.

"I know she's alive! I know she's alive! You must go get her. I hear her calling me!"

"It's okay, Mother. It's okay." The father looked at the son, and his eyes were filled with fright.

"Go get the whiskey," his father whispered.

The son went into the kitchen. The mother screamed again, "You must go dig her up! She's alive! I hear her calling!"

She would not touch the whiskey. The father and son stayed with her throughout the long night. When the day came she was still screaming, begging, and pleading, "Please, please, please, go get her!"

"Get her!"

The father turned to the son and said, "We must do it. We have got to show her, or she will never get better."

The three of them slipped away into the morning. The father and the son dug the grave, and the mother stood above them weeping and watching. The wind swept through her long gray hair and made shadows on the earth. Finally the shovel touched the box. They worked ropes under it and pulled it up. The father took the end of the shovel and began to pry open the lid. The very nails he had nailed down just the day before squeaked and strained, but finally he worked the coffin lid loose.

The father looked at the mother then he slowly lifted the lid of the coffin. The father dropped the shovel and stepped back! The mother shook her head and shrieked. The son fell to his knees in the dirt.

She lay quiet. Her dress was torn at the neck, and her face, no longer beautiful, was contorted and twisted with past pain. Her fingertips were covered with blood. The end of her finger-nails were gone. The plaid cotton lining of the coffin was shredded. And there were fingernail marks deeply carved in the wood underneath.

# STORY OUTLINE

I.   The beautiful daughter takes ill and dies, causing her family much grief.

II.  They bury her in a plaid-lined cedar box in the family cemetery.

III. The son hears horrible screams in the night and eventually learns that it is his mother. She demands that they dig up the coffin as she knows her daughter is alive.

IV.  The son and father dig up the grave early the next morning—but much to their horror the lining of the coffin has been shredded, with the girl's fingernail marks deeply carved into the wood because she had been buried alive!

# THE BLOODY HAND

as told by William Forgey

This anonymous legend was gleaned from a book of ghost stories. Generally these short stories do not lend themselves well to campfire telling, but I found this to be an exception.

n a certain village on the south coast, a widow and her two daughters were living in a house that stood rather apart from its neighbors on either side. It was situated on a wooded cliff, and about a quarter of a mile from its garden was a waterfall of some height. The two daughters were much attached to each other. One of them, Mary, was very attractive. Among her admirers there were two men especially distinguished for their devotion to her. One of them, John Bodneys, seemed on the point of realizing the ambition of his life when a new competitor of a very different disposition appeared and completely conquered Mary's heart.

The day was fixed for the marriage, but though Mary wrote to the Bodneys family to announce her engagement and to ask John to be present at her wedding, she had received no reply from him. On the evening before the wedding day, Ellen, the other sister was gathering ferns in the woods when she heard a faint rustling behind her and, turning quickly round, thought she had a momentary glimpse of the figure of John Bodneys. Whomever it was vanished swiftly in the twilight. On her return to the house, Ellen told her sister what she thought she had seen, but neither of them thought much of it.

The marriage took place next day. Just before the bride was due to leave with her husband, she took her sister to the room they had shared. It had a window that opened onto a balcony from which a flight of steps led down to the enclosed garden. After a few words, Mary said to her sister, "I would like to be alone for a few minutes. I will join you again presently."

Ellen left her and went downstairs where she waited with the others. When half an hour had passed and Mary had not appeared, her sister went up to see if anything had happened to her. The bedroom door was locked. Ellen called but had no answer. Becoming alarmed, she ran downstairs and told her mother. At last the door was forced open, but there was no trace of Mary in the room. They went into the garden, but except for a white rose lying on the path, nothing was to be seen. For the rest of that day and on the following days, they hunted for Mary high and low. The police were called in, the whole countryside was roused, but all to no purpose. Mary had utterly disappeared.

The years passed by. The mother and Mary's husband were dead, and of the wedding party only Ellen and an old servant were still alive. One winter's night the wind rose to a furious gale and did a great deal of damage to the trees near the waterfall. When workers came in the morning to clear away the fallen timber and fragments of rock, they found a skeleton hand, on the third finger of which was a wedding ring, guarded by another ring with a red stone in it. On searching further they found a complete skeleton, around whose bones some rags of clothes still adhered. The ring with the red stone in it was identified by Ellen as one that her sister was wearing on her wedding day. The skeleton was buried in the churchyard, but the shock of the discovery was so great that a few weeks later Ellen herself was on her deathbed. On the occasion of Mary's burial, she had insisted on keeping the skeleton hand with the rings, putting it in a glass box to secure it from accident. Now as she lay dying, she left the relic to the care of her old servant.

Shortly afterward the servant set up a hotel, where, as may

be imagined, the skeleton hand and its story were a common topic of conversation among those who frequented its bar. One night a stranger, muffled up in a cloak, with a cap pulled over his face, made his way into the inn and asked for something to drink.

"It was a night like this when the great oak was blown down," the bartender observed to one of his customers.

"Yes," the other replied. "And it must have made the skeleton seem doubly ghastly, discovering it, as it were, in the midst of ruins."

"What skeleton?" asked the stranger, turning suddenly from the corner in which he had been standing.

"Oh, it's a long story," answered the publican. "You can see the hand in that glass case, and if you like, I will tell you how it came to be there."

He waited for the stranger's answer, but none came. He was leaning against the wall in a state of collapse. He was staring at the hand, repeating again and again, "Blood, blood," and sure enough, blood was slowly dripping from his fingertips. A few minutes later, he had recovered sufficiently to admit that he was John Bodneys and to ask that he might be taken to the magistrates. He confessed to them that in a frenzy of jealousy, he had made his way into the private garden on Mary's wedding day. Seeing her alone in her room, he had entered and seized her, muffling her cries, and had taken her as far as the waterfall. There she had struggled so violently to escape from him that, unintentionally, he had pushed her off the rocks, and she had fallen into a cleft, where she was almost completely hidden. Afraid of being discovered, he had not even waited to find out whether she were dead or alive. He had fled and lived abroad ever since, until an overpowering longing led him to revisit the scene of his crime.

After making his confession, Bodneys was committed to the county jail, where shortly afterward he died, before any trial could take place.

# STORY OUTLINE

I.   John Bodneys was very attracted to Mary, but she fell in love with someone else. She invited John to her wedding, but he did not reply.

II.  Just before the bride was to leave with her husband, she went upstairs to her room. But she never came down! A search failed to find her.

III. Years passed and everyone who had been at the wedding had died but her sister and an old servant lady. A storm destroyed a large tree, whose roots pulled up the remains of a woman in wedding clothes, with a wedding ring on her skeleton hand. The body was identified as Mary's.

IV.  The body was buried in the churchyard, but her sister had kept the hand with its rings in a glass case. She soon died and left the hand to the old servant.

V.   The servant opened a tavern and hotel and displayed the hand in a glass case.

VI.    One day a stranger who overheard a conversation about the skeleton hand asked about it—the stranger stared at the hand and collapsed.

VII.   He admitted to being John Bodneys and to having killed Mary, leaving her in the crevasse by the old tree.

*When telling this story, I do not have the hand dripping blood, as in the original version, but rather have John Bodneys recognize the rings and the hand as belonging to the murder victim and collapsing because of this grisly reminder from his past.*

# ONE SUMMER NIGHT

by Ambrose Bierce

This tale by the macabre Bierce is about a topic that all medical students have had to encounter—the dead body required for dissection in anatomy class. In medieval Europe a copy of the keys to the city cemetery was a legacy passed from one medical school class to the next. Voluntary donations have now replaced body snatching, but this tale returns to the time—not so long ago—when medical students had to fend for themselves in this grisly business.

The fact that Henry Armstrong was buried did not seem to him to prove that he was dead: he had always been a hard man to convince. That he really was buried, the testimony of his senses compelled him to admit. His posture—flat upon his back, with his hands crossed upon his stomach and tied with something that he easily broke without profitably altering the situation—the strict confinement of his entire person, the black darkness and profound silence, made a body of evidence impossible to controvert and he accepted it without cavil.

But dead—no; he was only very, very ill. He had, withal, the invalid's apathy and did not greatly concern himself about the uncommon fate that had been allotted to him. No philosopher was he—just a plain, commonplace person gifted, for the time being, with a pathological indifference: the organ that he feared consequences with was torpid. So, with no particular apprehension for his immediate future, he fell asleep and all was peace with Henry Armstrong.

But something was going on overhead. It was a dark summer night, shot through with infrequent shimmers of lightning silently firing a cloud lying low in the west and portending a storm. These brief, stammering illuminations brought out with ghastly distinctness the monuments and headstones of the cemetery and seemed to set them dancing. It was not a night in which any credible witness was likely to be straying about a cemetery, so the three men who were there, digging into the grave of Henry Armstrong, felt reasonably secure.

Two of them were young students from a medical college a

few miles away; the third was a gigantic Negro known as Jess. For many years Jess had been employed about the cemetery as a man-of-all-work and it was his favorite pleasantry that he knew "every soul in the place." From the nature of what he was now doing it was inferable that the place was not so populous as its register may have shown it to be.

Outside the wall, at the part of the grounds farthest from the public road, were a horse and a light wagon, waiting.

The work of excavation was not difficult: the earth with which the grave had been loosely filled a few hours before offered little resistance and was soon thrown out. Removal of the casket from its box was less easy, but it was taken out, for it was a perquisite of Jess, who carefully unscrewed the cover and laid it aside, exposing the body in black trousers and white shirt. At that instant the air sprang to flame, a cracking shock of thunder shook the stunned world and Henry Armstrong tranquilly sat up. With inarticulate cries the men fled in terror, each in a different direction. For nothing on earth could two of them have been persuaded to return. But Jess was of another breed.

In the gray of the morning the two students, pallid and haggard from anxiety and with the terror of their adventure still beating tumultuously in their blood, met at the medical college.

"You saw it?" cried one.

"God! Yes—what are we to do?"

They went around to the rear of the building, where they saw a horse, attached to a light wagon, hitched to a gate post near the door of the dissecting room. Mechanically they entered the room. On a bench in the obscurity sat Jess. He rose, grinning, all eyes and teeth.

"I'm waiting for my pay," he said.

Stretched naked on a long table lay the body of Henry Armstrong, the head defiled with blood and clay from a blow with a spade.

# STORY OUTLINE

I.   Henry Armstrong was very ill and had been buried alive—he could tell that when he awoke.

II.  Up above him it was a dark night, complete with flashes of summer lightning. Three men were in the cemetery, digging up the grave of Henry Armstrong. Two were medical students, the other was a big fellow named Jess who was employed at the cemetery—a person who had stolen bodies often.

III. It was easy digging into the newly dug grave. Lifting the coffin out was less easy.

IV.  When the lid was removed, a crack of thunder shook the air—and Henry Armstrong sat up in the coffin.

V.   The three men ran in terror in different directions. The medical students met at the college early in the morning, still scared and haggard from their horrible night.

VI.    They went to the dissecting room, and there was Jess who said, "I'm waiting for my pay."

VII.   And on the table was the body of Henry Armstrong, his head crushed from a blow with a spade.

# THE FORK

by William Forgey

*This tale is the story of two friends who head into the wilderness, only to watch differences and idiosyncrasies drive them apart. It's really strange how easily this happens in the bush. The great outdoorsman and writer, Calvin Rutstrum, turned to me one day and said, "How do you tell your partner you hate his guts by the way he holds his fork?" That statement formed the basis for this story.*

Scott and Dave were lucky. Or at least they started out feeling very lucky. They were deeper into the north woods than they had ever been in their life, at a remote cabin, 120 miles from the town of Churchill, Manitoba, a small town located halfway up the east coast of Hudson Bay. Scott was the Junior Assistant Scoutmaster of Troop 16 and Dave was the Senior Patrol Leader. Scott's dad had arranged for the boys to fly in to a small lake about 3 miles from the cabin and to spend ten days there over Christmas vacation, after which Ernie, a trapper who lived in Churchill, was to arrive by snowmobile to bring them out.

The cabin was located at the very edge of the tree line. For thousands of miles north of them there was nothing but Arctic muskeg, "the barrens" as it is often called, while to the south a thousand miles of forest stretched to the plains of southern Canada and the U.S. border.

This cabin would have also been in the barrens except that it was in a valley that had protected the local trees from severe blasts of arctic cold, which would have prevented their growth, as it had done on the plateau above.

The incredible cold of this Canadian arctic land made the remoteness even more impressive. In fact survival would not be possible without the down parkas and pants, heavy wool clothing, and "polypro" underwear that Scott and Dave were wearing. But the cabin made the country not only safer to stay in, but allowed them to enjoy their adventure.

And what a cabin! Cut from local black spruce logs, the 12-foot-square building had a sleeping loft, a wood-burning stove, and a storage room that made the place appear like a palace in the north woods. To prevent cold from leaking in, the cabin only had one small window on the ground floor, but two Plexiglas windows had been installed in the sleeping loft to catch the early morning and afternoon light.

Catching light was important, for there is little of it at that time of year in northern Manitoba. The sun would peak above the horizon at 8:30 in the morning, then stay low on the southern horizon until it set by 2:30 in the afternoon. The rest of the time kerosene lights and the flickering light from the wood stove was the cabin's only source of light—unless Scott and Dave were outside after dark when the snow would reflect moonlight and frequent incredible displays of northern lights would fill the entire sky with curtains of mysterious, flickering fire.

What an adventure! The plane flight in from Churchill allowed them a glimpse of the 100 miles of frozen barrens that they would soon be dog sledding over. And then the edge of the forest with the tiny cabin tucked into the Windigo River Valley finally appeared through the frosted windows of the plane.

The pilot buzzed the cabin, but they could not tell from the snow-covered mound whether it was okay or not. He swooped twice more over the river, checking out landing conditions before setting the plane down, actually bumping to a stop only a few hundred feet from a gap in the trees near a path that probably led to the cabin.

Scott and Dave's excitement at first stepping out of the plane was matched only by their hushed expectations as they snowshoed their way to the long-abandoned cabin's door, hoping that the building was intact and habitable, allowing them to continue their great adventure. If it was not, they would have to call it off.

The pilot went with them. The quiet of the frozen north was impressive after the engine noise on the hour and a half flight from Churchill. The only sounds were the crunch of snowshoes against the frozen snow and the excited puffing of their breaths as they bound up the bank to the cabin site. The cabin was located only a short distance from the stream, but hidden by the trees well enough that it couldn't be seen easily. As they approached the cabin, they could see that the stove pipe was intact and the shutters were still fastened over the lower window. The Plexiglas windows in the sleeping loft above looked okay.

They removed the large crowbar used to barricade the door—for in the tradition of the north country this cabin had no lock. The barricade was there to prevent animals from easily shoving the door open.

As they peered into the dark, empty cabin, they could see that nothing had been disturbed. There was no mess from animal destruction, the walls still had their chinking, the wood stove and its flue looked functional, and a variety of lamps, parts, and various tools were all in their proper places.

The pilot returned to the plane with the boys and helped them unload their equipment. They had kerosene, winter sleeping bags, extra clothes, a .30-30 Winchester rifle and a 12 gauge shotgun, enough food to last the ten days until Ernie arrived and for the three-day snowmobile trip back to town— even extra gasoline for the return trip. The pilot was anxious to be off before his engine froze, possibly adding him to the guest list. And the boys were also eager for him to depart so that they could be on their own, away from all traces of civilization.

There was much to do at first. The shutters had to be taken down, the frozen pile of firewood uncovered, a water hole cut through 3 feet of river ice, and the stove started to heat the cabin. It was impossible to work with bare hands—the temperature hovered at 20 degrees below zero!

With all of the hustle and bustle of their first day in the bush, it wasn't long before 2:30 came and the sun set. The boys enjoyed their first meal in the bush—a beef stew they had allowed to cook nearly all day on the hot wood stove. That evening they stood beside the river's edge. The Windigo River seemed much wider at night. They could barely see the dark splotch of the waterhole against the pristine snow. And because they had been too busy to explore that day, there were no other tracks that they could see in the fresh snow. While they stood beside the river, a dim yellow light began to glow above the stunted tree growth, slowly creeping higher in the sky. Their excitement grew as they witnessed a strange and eerie phenomenon. As it grew stronger and more intense, the wavering light soared overhead, dancing wildly like a long silk scarf in a breeze. Swirls and whirlpools of light oozed from its depths, while the shimmering enchantment danced across the sky in a florescent glow.

They stood in awe, almost in disbelief. Troops of bright yellow spears began marching vertically toward the west. After a time the light began to fade, hanging in the heavens motionless, dissolving. The boys had witnessed their first grand display of the northern lights.

It was more than the remoteness, the cold, and the unusual natural phenomena that gave Scott and Dave a strange thrill as they stood there that night. The cabin they were being allowed to use was almost never occupied. And for a reason:

No Indian or white man would trap or live there, for it stood in a mysterious area. The very name of the river, Windigo, was a warning of the awe in which this area was held by the persons who named it. The Windigo creature is known in nearly every northern Indian legend, sometimes the name is translated as "he who walks on water and eats human bones." The myths about the Windigo were known by tribes as far south as Illinois.

"Tomorrow we will get breakfast before daylight so we can start to explore this area," Dave remarked, as much to himself as to his companion.

Scott voiced his agreement. The short hours of daylight were too precious to be wasting inside cooking. There was much to do outside—and exploring this countryside, especially looking for tracks to examine, the signs of the animal life that surrounded them, was high on the priority list. They felt certain that many unseen eyes were watching them. It would be nice to learn more about those eyes by examining the tracks in the snow tomorrow.

As the boys banked the stove and then snuggled into their sleeping bags in the loft, they were only vaguely aware of a muffled sound coming from the river.

Scott's wrist watch alarm went off the next morning at 7:00 A.M., otherwise they would have surely overslept. It was hard getting up. The cabin temperature had dropped because the stove fire had died many hours before. Shinning a light at the thermometer attached by a bracket outside the loft window, Scott could see that it was 38 degrees below zero! Muffled sounds had continued from the river all night. Dave had remarked that he was sure that it was the heaving of the frozen ice, as it cracked beneath the snow because of the intense cold.

**161**

They used the same fire that heated their cabin to a comfortable temperature to cook their breakfast of Red River cereal, a traditional north country breakfast that they had purchased in Winnipeg. The boys also prepared extra coffee for the trail and packed away hunks of fruitcake, beef sausage sticks, and pilot biscuits for a trail lunch.

They left the cabin just as the sun was glowing over the southeast horizon; the temperature had not warmed at all. Even getting into the snowshoes was an adventure, requiring quick work and many pauses to warm their fingers. But soon they were plowing their way through the snow, crossing the river, with plumes of frozen breath hanging behind them in the still, cold air.

They found just what they hoped they would see across the river. An incredible record of the otherwise invisible wildlife written in the snow. Not a creature was stirring in the bitter cold, but the tracks of their recent activity gave away their presence. It was apparent that there had been martin, mink, and considerable movement of spruce grouse in the woods. They also discovered a fox trail. But they were not just looking at trails. They had also brought sleds and a bow saw and axes; they needed to cut more firewood to replace what they were using from the cabin woodpile.

Each day they repeated the work required to live in the deep winter of the far north. Each night they huddled in the frozen cabin, listening to the strange muffled sounds of the deep wilderness. They were becoming more and more acclimatized to the bitter cold, a process that was to be important if they were to successfully tolerate the long snowmobile trip to Churchill.

As their trips took them farther afield, they were not only

seeing evidence of more and more species of wildlife, but also reading the dramas of life and death as they found several sites of recent kills marked by bloody, disheveled snow. These sights added to their fascination with the wild sounds that they could not quite grow accustomed to hearing each night, sounds drifting into their cabin from that frozen wilderness. They could not help but feel the wildness of the area. Perhaps it was the incredible remoteness or the evidence of death and the struggle for survival that was evident all around them, but without any doubt they were both feeling uneasy.

Call it what you will—the Windigo, the Manito—the remote wilderness had a spiritual component that was capable of drawing you deeper and deeper into itself. It was not entirely unpleasant, but the constant evidence of death, the survival of the fittest, also cast a sense of "evil" to the experience.

And that was the scary part. The mystery of this remote area had always had a fascination for both boys. They never quite understood why they were so strongly drawn to being in the outdoors. This wasn't simply being outdoors, however. They were deep in the heart of the outdoors, near the point of origin of the powerful pull that wild places had always exerted on them both.

After spending a week in this frozen wilderness, they could almost feel that civilization was a dream, and that what they were struggling with was the only reality of life. Dave particularly became fixated on the mysterious pull that this wildness seemed to generate, especially at night, while listening to the muted sounds of the groaning ice. Or was it ice?

Dave's solo sojourns into the night started with a simple ten-minute hike onto the river. His excuse was that he wanted to check out these night noises and confirm that they were coming from the river. The next night, however, he felt the need to go again, this time for half an hour. He knew it wasn't just to feel the ice rumble, but to be closer to the wildness all around him. To feel even more a part of it.

Scott, however, was looking forward to the snowmobile trip more and more. It would be an adventure in itself and would break the drudgery of daily life in the cabin; more importantly, deep inside he was beginning to long for a link with humans again, to long for a break from the wildness of the frozen forest.

On the third night that Dave went out, he was gone for almost an hour and a half. Scott was concerned for his own safety—who wants to be left alone in the north? But also genuinely worried about what was going on with Dave. And Dave gave very little explanation for the length of his absence on his return. He seemed almost mesmerized by the beckoning call of this wild place. And that's when they had their big argument.

Dave and Scott were very good friends before this trip; they had made many trips together. But Scott's annoyance with Dave's wandering started to expand into other areas. Perhaps he felt he was being abandoned, that by traveling alone Dave was taking risks that would threaten both their safety. Regardless he started noticing other aggravating traits that Dave had. For example, the way Dave brushed his teeth and then spit the water out between his front teeth. At first this was nothing, but as the tension mounted, it somehow became annoying.

Then there was the matter of how Dave so thoroughly cleaned his plate. Everyone is hungry during a wilderness trip.

There never seems to be enough food. But Dave would literally scrape his plate clean with his fork. Scrape, scrape, scrape. Finally Scott had just about had it watching this happen with every meal.

How do you tell your partner you hate his guts because of the way he holds his fork?

Tension like this is without a doubt contagious. So Dave's strong attachment to the call of the wild seemed to accelerate, partially to serve a selfish purpose, to enjoy the wilderness, partially to get away from the tension in the cabin.

And Scott's opinion of all of this? "Good, I'm glad the Windigo is calling him. Maybe it will teach him how to eat properly!"

But on the fourth night Dave did not return at all.

When Scott awoke at 4:00 A.M. and found himself alone, he felt a sudden cold chill that even the bitter temperature could not account for strike him. He had another five hours before daylight, so he started a fire to warm the icy cabin, hoping the light and warmth would ease the fear in his heart. But, of course it did not.

Alone on the edge of the barrens. The more he thought about it, the more he realized how much Dave had been changing. He had seemed more than just interested in the wilderness. He had become captured by it. It was as if the Windigo itself was achieving a presence within Dave. And that damned fork!

But even having that thought, Scott became more concerned about Dave. He could hardly wait for the sun to come up so that he could go out to look for him. The wind had been gradually building. The snow had started blowing off the arctic plateau above them, dumping larger and larger amounts into the valley. The five hours was like five years. But finally the glow brightened and a gray, stormy day dawned. Scott immediately saw that it would be impossible to attempt to find Dave. The continuing storm made travel impossible. The wild seemed to have swallowed Dave whole.

And thus he spent the day alone. While the wilderness seemed to call to Dave, it was doing the very opposite to Scott. He was feeling crushed by it. He wanted to stay in the cabin and was reluctant to go outside at all.

A cabin can be a place of refuge in the wilderness, but it can also easily become a prison. And although being in prison would be a horrible experience, it paled compared with the position that Scott was in. His best friend, and the only other human in this vast wilderness, Dave, had disappeared, leaving him alone. He feared for Dave—and he feared for himself. He did not know which of these emotions was the strongest. There is the "cut to the quick" fear that one has for one's own survival, possibly nothing is stronger than that. But if there is another stronger fear, it is the fear that something has happened to your best friend. And when that best friend is also your only link to civilization, it intensifies the combination of personal danger and grief that one could feel. And imagine experiencing all of this alone.

Eventually the long night came to a close—daybreak arrived. It was the day that Ernie was to arrive. The day that was to be the start of another adventure had come to represent something much more basic: raw survival. Scott's strongest desire was just to get out of this place. After that it was not knowing where Dave was or what happened to him.

Finally Scott heard the distant noise of a snow machine, the powerful snowmobile that Ernie was driving. The sounds rose and fell, seeming at one moment close and the next far away, until finally there was the consistent racket of the powerful machine grinding its way up the river near the cabin.

It stopped outside the cabin. The commotion was replaced first by silence, and then the soft crunching of footsteps in the snow making their way around the side of the cabin to the front door.

Scott waited with bated breath until suddenly the door burst open, and Ernie stood there with a great grin on his face.

"How ya doing here, eh? Bet you're getting a bit lonely!" he exclaimed.

Because he saw how Scott was sitting, more or less cowering, dumbfounded, in the corner by the table, he immediately added, "Well, I brought a present for you!"

Scott could hardly make sense of what he heard. He was safe! But his partner was gone.

"I found him about 6 miles out, near the junction with the Churchill River, all cuddled up in a snow cave. Bet you thought the Manito got 'em, eh?"

And with that Dave crunched his way through the door. "Hi Scott! I never thought I'd be so glad to see another person this much in my life! I'm sorry I got carried away with the pull of the wilderness. It really taught me a lesson. I'm sorry that I pulled that stunt and left you here alone."

And Scott, feeling the same way, knew that he had been given a great present, indeed. He was so very thankful that Dave was alive and that he was no longer alone. But he never wanted to have to watch David eat with a fork again.

# STORY OUTLINE

I.     Dave and Scott fly to a remote cabin on the Windigo River in Northern Manitoba to spend ten days, before being joined by Ernie with a snowmobile for the return trip to Churchill.

II.     The mysterious wilderness exerts a pull on Dave, causing him to travel alone to enjoy it better.

III.     Scott feels the stress of the lonesome wilderness and soon starts to notice minor problems with Dave's mannerisms.

IV.     Finally Scott concentrates on Dave's use of his fork, and it starts to drive him nuts. ("How do you tell your partner you hate his guts because of the way he holds his fork?")

V.     Dave disappears into a storm one night, and Scott is left alone. Scott feels sorry that his relationship with Dave has deteriorated over such minor things, but also feels the fear of being alone and anger at Dave for having put him into this situation.

VI.     Ernie arrives with the snowmobile; he has found Dave, who was in a snow cave seeking refuge from the storm.

VII.   Scott is thankful that his best friend is safe, but he never wants to watch him eat with a fork again!

# THE STRANGER

by Ambrose Bierce

*Some of Ambrose Bierce's tales of the supernatural make particularly good campfire stories—especially this one with its outdoors setting, around a campfire in remote wilderness, about someone—or something—that entered this group's lives.*

A man stepped out of the darkness into the little illuminated circle about our failing campfire and seated himself upon a rock.

"You are not the first to explore this region," he said gravely.

Nobody controverted his statement; he was himself proof of its truth, for he was not of our party and must have been somewhere near when we camped. Moreover, he must have companions not far away; it was not a place where one would be living or traveling alone. For more than a week we had seen, besides ourselves and our animals, only such living things as rattlesnakes and horned toads. In an Arizona desert one does not long coexist with only such creatures as these; one must have pack animals, supplies, arms—"an outfit." And all these imply comrades. It was, perhaps, a doubt as to what manner of men this unceremonious stranger's comrades might be, together with something in his words interpretable as a challenge, that caused every man of our half-dozen "gentlemen adventurers" to rise to a sitting posture and lay his hand upon a weapon—an act signifying, in that time and place, a policy of expectation. The stranger gave the matter no attention, and began again to speak in the same deliberate, uninflected monotone in which he had delivered his first sentence:

"Thirty years ago Ramon Gallegos, William Shaw, George W. Kent and Berry Davis, all of Tucson, crossed the Santa Catalina Mountains and traveled due west, as nearly as the configuration of the country permitted. We were prospecting and it was our intention, if we found nothing, to push through to the Gila River at some point near Big Bend, where we understood there was a settlement. We had a good outfit but no guide, just Ramon Gallegos, William Shaw, George W. Kent and Berry Davis."

The man repeated the names slowly and distinctly, as if to fix them in the memories of his audience, every member of which was now attentively observing him, but with a slack- ened apprehension regarding his possible companions some- where in the darkness which seemed to enclose us like a black wall, for in the manner of this volunteer historian was no suggestion of an unfriendly purpose. His act was rather that of a harmless lunatic than an enemy. We were not so new to the country as not to know that the solitary life of many a plainsman had a tendency to develop eccentricities of con- duct and character not always easily distinguishable from mental aberration. A man is like a tree: in a forest of his fel- lows he will grow as straight as his genetic and individual nature permits; alone, in the open, he yields to the deforming stresses and tortions that environ him. Some such thoughts were in my mind as I watched the man from the shadow of my hat, pulled low to shut out the firelight. A witless fellow, no doubt, but what could he be doing there in the heart of a desert?

Nobody having broken the silence, the visitor went on to say: "This country was not then what it is now. There was not a ranch between the Gila and the Gulf. There was a little game here and there in the mountains, and near the infre- quent water holes grass enough to keep our animals from starvation. If we should be so fortunate as to encounter no Indians, we might get through. But within a week the purpose of the expedition had altered from discovery of wealth to preservation of life. We had gone too far to go back, for what was ahead could be no worse than what was behind; so we pushed on, riding by night to avoid Indians and the intolerable heat, and concealing ourselves by day as best we could. Sometimes, having exhausted our supply of wild meat and emptied our casks, we were days without food and drink; then a water hole or a shallow pool in the bottom of an arroyo so restored our strength and sanity that we were able to shoot some of the wild animals that sought it also. Sometimes it was a bear, sometimes an antelope, a coyote, a cougar—that was as God pleased; all were food.

"One morning as we skirted a mountain range, seeking a practicable pass, we were attacked by a band of Apaches who had followed our trail up a gulch—it is not far from here. Knowing that they outnumbered us ten to one, they took none of their usual cowardly precautions, but dashed upon us at a gallop, firing and yelling. Fighting was out of the question. We urged our feeble animals up the gulch as far as there was footing for a hoof, then threw ourselves out of our saddles and took to the chaparral on one of the slopes, abandoning our entire outfit to the enemy. But we retained our rifles, every man—Ramon Gallegos, William Shaw, George W. Kent, and Berry Davis."

"Same old crowd," said the humorist of the party. A gesture of disapproval from our leader silenced him, and the stranger proceeded with his tale:

"The savages dismounted also, and some of them ran up the gulch beyond the point at which we had left it, cutting off further retreat in that direction and forcing us on up the side. Unfortunately the chaparral extended only a short distance up the slope, and as we came into the open ground above we took the fire of a dozen rifles; but Apaches shoot badly when in a hurry, and God so willed it that none of us fell. Twenty yards up the slope, beyond the edge of the brush, were vertical cliffs, in which, directly in front of us, was a narrow opening. Into that we ran, finding ourselves in a cavern about as large as an ordinary room. Here for a time we were safe. A single man with a repeating rifle could defend the entrance against all the Apaches in the land. But against hunger and thirst we had no defense. Courage we still had, but hope was a memory.

"Not one of those Indians did we afterwards see, but by the smoke and glare of their fires in the gulch we knew that by day and by night they watched with ready rifles in the edge of the bush—knew that, if we made a sortie, not a man of us would live to take three steps into the open. For three days, watching in turn, we held out, before our suffering became insupportable. Then—it was the morning of the fourth day—Ramon Gallegos said,

" 'Señore, I know not well of the good God and what please him. I have lived without religion, and I am not acquainted with that of yours. Pardon, señores, if I shock you, but for me the time is come to beat the game of the Apache.'

"He knelt upon the rock floor of the cave and pressed his pistol against his temple. Madre de Dios,' he said, 'comes now the soul of Ramon Gallegos.'

"And so he left us—William Shaw, George W. Kent, and Berry Davis.

"I was the leader. It was for me to speak.

" 'He was a brave man,' I said. 'He knew when to die, and

how. It is foolish to go mad from thirst and fall by Apache bullets, or be skinned alive—it is in bad taste. Let us join Ramon Gallegos.'

" 'That is right,' said William Shaw.

" 'That is right,' said George W. Kent.

"I straightened the limbs of Ramon Gallegos and put a handkerchief over his face. Then William Shaw said: 'I should like to look like that a little while."

"And George W. Kent said that he felt that way too.

" 'It shall be so,' I said. 'The devils will wait a week. William Shaw and George W. Kent, draw and kneel.'

"They did so and I stood before them.

" 'Almighty God, our Father,' said I.

" 'Almighty God, our Father,' said William Shaw.

" 'Almighty God, our Father,' said George W. Kent.

" 'Forgive us our sins,' said I.

" 'Forgive us our sins,' said they.

" 'And receive our souls.'

" 'And receive our souls.'

" 'Amen!'

" 'Amen!'

"I laid them beside Ramon Gallegos and covered their faces."

There was a quick commotion on the opposite side of the campfire. One of our party had sprung to his feet, pistol in hand.

"And you!" he shouted, "you dared to escape?—you dare to be alive? You cowardly hound, I'll send you to join them if I hang for it!"

But with the leap of a panther the captain was upon him, grasping his wrist. "Hold it in, Sam Yountsey, hold it in!"

We were now all upon our feet, except the stranger, who sat motionless and apparently inattentive. Someone seized Yountsey's other arm.

"Captain," I said, "there is something wrong here. This fellow is either a lunatic or merely a liar—just a plain, everyday liar that Yountsey has no call to kill. If this man was of that party it had five members, one of whom—probably himself—he has not named."

"Yes," said the captain, releasing the insurgent, who sat down, "there is something—unusual. Years ago four dead bodies of white men, scalped and shamefully mutilated, were found about the mouth of that cave. They are buried there; I have seen the graves—we shall all see them tomorrow."

The stranger rose, standing tall in the light of the expiring fire, which in our breathless attention to his story we had neglected to keep going.

"There were four," he said. "Ramon Gallegos, William Shaw, George W. Kent, and Berry Davis."

With this reiterated roll call of the dead he walked into the darkness and we saw him no more.

At that moment one of our party, who had been on guard, strode in among us, rifle in hand and somewhat excited.

"Captain," he said, "for the last half-hour three men have been standing out there on the mesa." He pointed in the direction taken by the stranger. "I could see them distinctly, for the moon is up, but as they had no guns and I had them covered with mine, I thought it was their move. They have made none, but damn it! They got on my nerves."

"Go back to your post, and stay till you see them again," said the captain. "The rest of you lie down again, or I'll kick you all into the fire."

The sentinel obediently withdrew, swearing, and did not return. As we were arranging our blankets, the fiery Yountsey said: "I beg your pardon, Captain, but who the devil do you take them to be?"

"Ramon Gallegos, William Shaw, and George W. Kent."

"But how about Berry Davis? I ought to have shot him."

"Quite needless; you couldn't have made him any deader. Go to sleep."

*The original story glosses over the fact that Berry Davis sat with the dead bodies of his friends a full week before he killed himself, so that his friend could rest unmutilated by Indians "for a little while" as requested by William Shaw and George W. Kent. I generally make more a point of this when telling the story—actually drawing out his staying in the hot cave with his dead friends, holding off the Indians' attacks, and starving until he could stand it no longer—then killing himself.*

# STORY OUTLINE

I.  A group of cowboys was seated around a campfire in Arizona when a stranger stepped into the light of their fire and told them a story.

II. He related how Ramon Gallegos, William Shaw, George W. Kent, and Berry Davis had been prospecting in that area many years before.

III.     They nearly starved and died from thirst as they struggled through the unexplored desert, shooting what game they could find at water holes.

IV.     They traveled by night to avoid the heat and Indians, but their luck ran out one morning when a band of Apaches caught up with them and trapped them in a gully.

V.      The men found refuge from Indian bullets in a cave but were trapped without food or water.

VI.     After three days they could stand it no longer and Ramon Gallegos said he did not want to be tortured by thirst and hunger and shot himself.

VII.    His body was laid out with a handkerchief over his face. William Shaw and George W. Kent said that they would like to look like that without being mutilated by the Indians, if only for a little while. Their leader said, "It shall be so. I will make the devils wait a week before they get your bodies."

VIII.   The two men were laid out alongside Ramon Gallegos, their faces covered.

IX.     Some of the cowboys thought that this man had escaped the massacre and had abandoned his friends, or that he was a fifth member of this group.

X.   The cowboy foreman said that four mutilated bodies had been found at a cave entrance near where they were camping many years ago, and that their graves were close by.

XI.   The stranger repeated that there were only four in the party—and again gave their names. He then left the camp.

XII.   The guard came in and said he had noted three men just standing outside of their camp. He was told to return to his guard duty, and the rest of the men were ordered to bed.

XIII.   The foreman was asked who the three men were, and he answered, "Ramon Gallegos, William Shaw, and George W. Kent." When a cowboy said he should have shot the cowardly Berry Davis, the foreman answered, "Quite needless; you couldn't have made him any deader. Go to sleep."

*If you have trouble remembering the slain men's names, try substituting the names of relatives or coworkers.*

# THE MANOR

as told by Pat Sherwood

*This story is an adaptation of an old Sir Walter Scott story by the same name. It has been placed in a modern setting to provide more relevance for the campfire audience. Some old stories, such as "The Stranger," are best left in their ancient settings, while others seem to work better with modernization.*

The road and the scenery whizzed by, but the country's beauty was lost to the driver. His thoughts weren't on the local charms or even on the destination for which the car was headed, his mind was on a war, a war in a faraway land.

But the war was over for Lt. Col. Brad Rallings, at least the combat was over. A Viet Cong land mine had seen to that. It was strange the way things had turned out. He was one of the few that had become exactly what he had always wanted to be, a combat officer. Now he would finish his career behind a desk at a training command, a career that had taken him through four tours of Viet Nam, earned him a chest full of medals and now a leg that would never function as it should again. Yeah, it was strange the way things turn out sometimes.

A sudden curve in the road brought him back to reality, and the colonel took notice of the picturesque countryside that was all around him. His thoughts turned to his destination and a friend he had not seen since he first entered the service. It would be great seeing his childhood buddy again. He and Ken had been chums since they were old enough to walk. They did everything together. They were even roommates in college. Ken went into business and Brad entered the military. But they had always kept in contact with each other, no matter where their careers took them.

Ken had inherited an old country manor a few years back. Actually it was more of an estate. Ken had converted it into a resort, the opening of which occurred just a few weeks earlier. Now that the colonel had several weeks of medical leave, he couldn't think of a better place to recuperate than at a quiet manor out in the country. Three weeks of total peace and quiet would hopefully give him a new frame of mind with regard to his new command behind a desk.

The road wound through the countryside like a shiny ribbon, enshrouded on either side by thick green woods, which, from time to time, gave way at different points to offer the eye a fleeting glimpse of the truly magnificent scenery. It was through one of these woodland portholes that the colonel first caught sight of the manor. The colonel stopped his car and gazed across the valley at the manor resting sedately on the side of the adjacent hill. The sight was enough to bring a sense of calm to the haggard soldier's mind. His heart warmed at the thought of his lifelong friend in possession of such a delightful place. He couldn't picture a better place to rest up before returning to his duties as a soldier. He quickly pulled away, now anxious to see his friend and get settled in for a much needed rest.

On his arrival the colonel was greeted by a porter, who when learning his identity, quickly sent word of his arrival to the owner. As he waited, the colonel looked about in awe. The manor was even more splendid than he had imagined. It was then that the colonel first saw Ken, and although the years had been many, he instantly recognized him. But for a moment his childhood friend seemed to hesitate and looked at him like a stranger. Colonel Rallings had the face of a soldier, upon which war with its fatigues and wounds had made a great alteration. But the uncertainty lasted only until the colonel spoke. The hearty greeting that followed was one that could only be shared between those who had spent countless days of childhood and early youth together.

"If I had but one wish," said the soldier's friend, "it would

be that you had been here to share the opening of my manor!"
Brad made a suitable reply and congratulated his friend on the
fine manor he had acquired. "You ain't seen nothing yet ole
buddy!" his friend replied and proceeded to give the colonel a
personally guided tour of the manor.

"Don't think that your exploits haven't been watched," Ken
told him at one point, "I've kept close track of your career and
a glorious one it's been. Twice decorated for valor, a
Distinguished Service Cross, and so many more honors that I
can't count them all."

The tour ended when they came to an isolated area of the
manor. The colonel's friend led him down a hallway that
ended in front of a large oak door that strangely did not
match the rest of the décor. "This is part of the original
manor," his friend explained, "It's much like it was when the
house was first built, and I've reserved it especially for you.
Now why don't you freshen up. I'll see you for dinner at about
eight in the dining room." With that the owner of the manor
took his leave.

The colonel found the room to be something right out of
the 1800s, with heavy ornate wood trim and plastered walls.
The furnishings were antique and centered around a very large
four-poster bed. All in all the room was quite nice and seemed
the perfect place to relax.

After unpacking the colonel took a stroll on the large balcony that ran the length of the manor and adjoined his room.
He had access to it by way of two large patio doors. He felt
relaxed and comfortable. The colonel looked forward to dinner with his friend.

A celebration took place that evening in the dining hall.
Ken had prepared a special banquet in the colonel's honor,

and it was attended by many of the owner's friends and guests. The soldier was introduced as a man of great honor and bravery. His exploits and awards were revealed to those attending, and the colonel was coaxed by his host to speak of his adventures. All who were present looked on the soldier as a brave officer, one who was sensible, cool under fire, and who had gained the respect of his fellow officers and the men who fought under him.

After dinner the evening turned to entertainment and dancing. The atmosphere was that of a relaxed party. The festivities ended at a respectable hour, and the guests returned to their rooms. The host accompanied the colonel to his room, and when they reached the door, he inquired if his friend found his accommodations to his liking. The colonel answered that it was most comfortable, and because it was the property of such a dear friend, he would rather be here than anywhere else. The two childhood friends bid each other good night with a warm handshake. "I'll see you at breakfast promptly at eight," his host said as he retreated down the hall.

The colonel entered his room, looked around, and thought to himself how different it was here, how comfortable compared with the hardships and pain he had suffered the past few weeks. With this he prepared himself for bed and a luxurious night's sleep.

The next morning found the host and a few friends assembled for breakfast at eight without the colonel. Because he was the desired guest, his absence was justly noticed. More than once Ken expressed his surprise at the soldier's lack of promptness and finally sent a porter to check on the colonel. The porter came back to inform him that the colonel was not in his room and had been seen walking about the terrace and grounds since very early that morning, which seemed strange because the weather had turned cold and misty.

"Just like a soldier," said the host to those around the table. "Many of them have the habit of not sleeping past light because their duty calls for them to be alert at early hours." But his explanation didn't really sit well with Ken, and he soon excused himself to find his boyhood friend. Ken found the colonel as the porter had said, roaming aimlessly about the grounds. The colonel looked extremely fatigued and fever-ish. His clothes were wrinkled and hung on him with a care-less negligence that was surprising for a military man. His hair was mussed and damp with dew, his face haggard and ghastly in some strange way.

"You look absolutely horrible this morning, Brad," com-mented Ken with some concern. "Are you feeling all right? Why were you wandering around so early this morning? You okay?"

"I'm fine," the colonel replied quickly, but with the air of embarrassment that made it obvious that he was not telling the truth.

"Why don't you come in and get a cup of coffee and eat some breakfast. You'll feel better," Ken said.

"No thanks, Ken," answered the colonel with a quiver in his voice. With a hesitation that didn't go unnoticed, the colonel said that he had asked the porter to collect his bags and bring his car around.

"Why?" asked Ken with surprise. "You said you'd spend at least a couple of weeks. Why the sudden change of heart?"

"I'm sorry, Ken. I know it's sudden, but I must get to my next command," announced the much decorated soldier with obvious embarrassment.

"That's a bunch of bull and you know it!" his friend said firmly. "Now level with me, what happened last night that has you so rattled?"

After a long hesitation, the colonel turned and looked into the eyes of the man with whom he had shared his childhood and who was undoubtedly his best friend. It was then that Ken noticed something he had never before seen in the eyes of this modern day warrior. He saw fear!

"Brad, as my oldest and dearest friend and on the honor of a soldier, I want you to answer me honestly, how did you sleep last night?" asked the owner of the manor.

There was once again a long hesitation. Then with a sigh of resignation, the brave colonel answered, "I've never in my life spent such a horrible night. It was so miserable that I couldn't run the risk of spending another night, not for anything, not even for you."

"This is unbelievable," said the host as if speaking to himself. Ken turned back to the colonel and said, "For God's sake Brad, be candid and tell me everything that happened last night. Tell me what could possibly have done this to you."

The colonel seemed very distressed by his friend's request and paused at length before he replied. "Ken, what happened last night was so bizarre and frightening that I wouldn't want to recount it to anybody, not even you. But I feel somehow honor bound to tell you what happened. If I told anyone else they would think I had completely flipped out, but you know me, and you should know that I would never make up something as unthinkable as what I'm about to tell you."

With this the colonel paused and looked directly into the eyes of his friend.

"Believe me Brad, I know there's something really bothering you. I know that you'll be telling the truth no matter how strange it sounds!" replied Ken. "Now tell me what happened."

"All right," said the veteran soldier, "I'll tell you as best I can, relying on your discretion; and yet I'd rather face a company of V.C. than recall what happened last night!"

The brave colonel paused again; Ken's silence confirmed his attention and willingness to hear him out. So with great reluctance and a sense of uneasiness, the colonel related the events of the worst night in his life.

"After you left me last night, I got ready for bed. The fire in the hearth burned brightly, and I lay thinking of our childhood and growing up, how our lives had changed over the years. All of these were fond memories. I was glad to be here, spending this time with my best friend." Again the colonel paused, then almost forcing himself, he continued. "I was just about to doze off, when I was aroused by the sound of footsteps, like that a woman would make in high heels as she walked across the floor. I could also hear the rustling of material, like a woman's gown would make. As I sat up in bed and focused my eyes, I saw the figure of a woman pass in front of the fireplace. Her back was to me, but by the way she held herself, her neck, her shoulders, I could tell that it was an old woman whose dress was an old-fashioned gown, like those you see in a movie about the Civil War."

The colonel closed his eyes for a moment, then cleared his throat to continue. "I really didn't think much of the intrusion. I figured it to be no more than an elderly (perhaps senile) guest who was confused as to the room in which she belonged. So I shifted myself to accommodate my injured leg and coughed to let her know I was there. That's when she slowly turned toward me. I swear, Ken, nothing in my life prepared me for what I saw." The soldier's eye looked skyward, and Ken could see the fear that was in them as his friend forced himself to continue. "There wasn't any doubt as to what she was, or even any chance that she was still among the living. Her face had the fixed features of a corpse, yet somehow manifested the vile, hideous passions she possessed while alive. Her form was like some demonic soul that the devil sent back from the grave! Some fiendish creature whose guilt was too great to lie quietly in eternity. In my horror I pushed myself backward to the head of the bed, supporting myself on my palms. Too scared to move, I watched as this hideous specter, in what seemed a single move, climbed right onto the bed. No more than a foot away from me, she squatted over the top of me. Her eyes were wide and wild, as if she was completely insane. Her grin was that of demonic maniac, mocking and full of malice."

Here the colonel stopped and wiped the cold beads of sweat that had formed during the recalling of that horrible night. His breathing was labored, and he tried to calm himself before he went on.

"My Lord, Ken," the colonel continued in a trembling voice. "I'm no coward. I've proven that a hundred times on the battlefield, and I've never dishonored myself or my men. But having this thing hovering over me with those horrible demonic eyes and being so close that . . . that horrid evil incarnation. . . ." He paused to recapture his labored breath. "I . . . I couldn't control my fear. My blood seemed to turn to ice. The hair stood up on the back of my neck, and I shook with panic . . . that's when I must have passed out."

The soldier's head seemed to fall in shame. When he again

spoke, his voice was weak and shaky, "How long I was out I couldn't tell you."

The haggard soldier, the person that Ken was sure possessed no fear, slowly walked a few steps and gazed out over the terrace, gathering himself before going on with his terrible story.

"When I finally came to, I lay with my eyes closed for some time for fear of seeing that horrible hag hovering above me once again. When I finally gathered enough courage to look, she was no longer there. It's to my own shame that I'll tell you, I was so afraid of crossing paths with that terrible creature again that I laid huddled in that bed, too afraid to get out. I can't even begin to tell you of the hideous things that ran through my mind as I lay there waiting for dawn. But those were all in my mind, I knew the difference. At first light of day I quickly threw on my clothes and got out of that haunted room. I wandered the grounds trying to soothe my nerves. Now you know why I can't spend another night under the same roof with that demon hag."

As strange as he colonel's tale was, Ken had no doubt as to the conviction in his friend's recollection of the previous night. He never questioned the possibility that it all could have been a bad dream. Quite the contrary, Ken didn't seem to doubt a single word of the soldier's tale. A look of sorrow and regret had taken over his normally jovial face.

"I'm truly sorry for the pain and anguish you have suffered," Ken began slowly, "for I'm afraid I'm to blame for what happened last night! That room I gave you last night has been closed up for many, many years because it was said to be haunted. When I inherited the manor, I reopened the room, not believing at all that it was haunted. Everybody around here knows of the room, and I figured that they would be biased toward it and rekindle the rumors if they were to spend the night there. So when you called and said you were coming, I thought it the perfect opportunity to dispel the rumors and make the room useful again. Your courage is indisputable, and with no prior knowledge of the room, you were perfect for my little experiment."

"Thanks a lot, Ken" said the colonel, somewhat hastily. "I'll be forever in your debt, as I'm likely to remember for some time the consequences of your so-called little experiment. Next time, find some other guinea pig!"

"Now you're being unfair, Brad," Ken said. "I would never have put you through that if for a moment I believed it would cause you so much grief. You know that. If I had told you ahead of time, you would have jumped at the chance to stay in that room. Perhaps I was wrong in my method, but what happened last night was not my fault. You must remember that until this morning, I honestly didn't believe that the room was haunted."

"You're right, Ken," said the colonel, the anger no longer in his voice. "I know I have no right to be mad at you. Until last night I didn't believe in ghosts either and most likely would have taken that room if you had told me. Look, I see that my car's here, and I don't want to keep you from your guests any longer, so I'll be going now."

"Brad, wait. I know there's no way I can talk you into remaining now, but can't you stay for a while? There are some things that I want to show you," pleaded the colonel's friend.

The shaken colonel accepted the invitation, although somewhat reluctantly. Brad Rallings would not breathe easy until he was far away from this manor, but he owed it to his lifelong friend to at least grant his request.

The colonel followed his host through several rooms and into a long gallery hung with portraits, which Ken pointed out were his ancestors and former owners of the manor. As they moved down the gallery, Ken would point out certain paintings, telling their names and giving some account of who they were. Colonel Rallings had little interest but followed along quietly. They were about halfway down the gallery when Ken noticed that the colonel suddenly stiffened and jumped back in the utmost surprise and not without some fear, if the way his eyes were riveted to a portrait of an old lady in a sacque, the fashionable dress of the end of the seventeenth century, were any indication.

"There she is!" he exclaimed. "That's her, the woman from the room! Not as hideous as last night, but it's her nonetheless!"

"If that's the case," said the colonel's friend, "there's no doubt as to the horrible reality of your ghost. That is a picture of a wretched ancestress of mine. Her crimes are too numerous to count, too horrible to name. Let's just say that the crimes committed in that room were unnatural acts of violence and death. I will reseal the room, leaving it to the isolation to which the better judgment of those before me consigned it; and never again, as long as I can help it, will anyone go through the anguish that you have."

Thus the two friends who had met with such happiness, parted in very different moods: Ken to dismantle the haunted room and have it sealed; and the colonel to finish out his career, hoping to forget that horrifying night he passed while at the manor.

# STORY OUTLINE

I.  A wounded Vietnam war hero, Lt. Col. Brad Rallings, was home on sick leave and planned to visit a high school friend, whom he had not seen for years.

II.  His friend, Ken, had inherited an old country manor and had turned it into a resort, inviting Brad to spend several weeks there to aid in his recuperation.

III.  Brad was the guest of honor at dinner. Everyone admired the war hero and gave him great respect because of his demonstrated heroism.

IV.  Ken took Brad to the special guest room that had been prepared for him, a room strangely isolated in an unused portion of the old manor house.

V.  The next morning the colonel failed to appear for breakfast. When Ken found him wandering outside, Brad appeared fatigued and rumpled.

VI.  Ken asked him how he slept and finally learned that the brave colonel had just spent the most terrifying night of his life.

VII.  Brad related that just as he was falling asleep, he had heard footsteps of a woman.

VIII. Brad could see an old woman pass between him and the fireplace. Thinking that she was a guest who had wandered accidentally into his room, he coughed to let her know he was there.

IX. But an evil, dead creature turned toward him and leaped upon his bed, causing him to feel such concentrated horror that he became paralyzed with fear and passed out.

X. When he awoke, he was afraid to open his eyes, fearing that the hideous face would still be hovering over him.

XI. He stayed frozen in fright until dawn appeared, when he immediately threw on his clothes and left the mansion to soothe his nerves.

XII. His friend apologized for placing him in the haunted room but pointed out that he need-ed someone with great courage, who had not heard of the ghost, to test the room and find the truth.

XIII. Ken then told Brad that he had to show him something. Taking him on a tour of the manor, he showed Brad a series of family portraits. Suddenly Brad recognized one as being that of the woman whose ghost he had seen he night before.

XIV. Ken told Brad that she had been an evil

wretch, and that she had committed horrible crimes in that room. He swore that he would seal the room forever so that no one would ever again have to experience the fear that Brad had.

# THE COMPANION

by Pat Sherwood

*As a scoutmaster, a hunter, and an outdoorsman, I've become accus-*
*tomed to being in the woods after dark, and I usually walk the trails*
*around my campsite without the aid of a light. I believe most people*
*who spend any amount of time in the outdoors grow to expect the*
*unexpected from time to time and condition themselves to deal with*
*such things. But even the most experienced outdoorsperson can't be*
*ready for everything.*

It was a moonless night in the latter part of August and the second night in camp for Troop 76. The fading embers of the campfire indicated the lateness of the night. All the scouts were safely tucked into their sleeping bags, and the leaders were just settling into theirs. The only one that remained outside was Dan, the troop's senior patrol leader. He had just finished checking the campsite and was now putting out the campfire. Being the top scout meant added responsibility, but Dan Livingston didn't mind. He was a born leader. It came naturally to him. After he finished, it was time to take a walk to the shower house and prepare for a night's rest. The troop had taken a campsite far back from the others in a primitive area of a state park, so he had to walk a good distance.

The cool, crisp air was filled with the scents and sounds of the night. Dan's thoughts were of the next day's events as he came upon the hard road that ran along a ridge that led to the main area of the campground. It was quite dark. He could just barely make out the outline of the road's edge. Dan had gone about 20 yards or so when it struck him that something had changed. It was much quieter than it had been only a few moments before. Suddenly, without cause or reason, a chill ran up the spine of the senior patrol leader. He was overtaken by a feeling of apprehension, some sense of foreboding that he couldn't justify. Dan knew he was tired and dismissed the feeling as silliness on his part, then continued on his way.

In the past Dan had stumbled on a lot of critters while roaming about the woods at night and some have given him quite a startle. The sudden rustling noise on the side of the

**201**

road gave him no real concern. It could've been most anything—perhaps a raccoon on its way to the main camp-
grounds for a late night snack from some camper's ice chest.

The rustling noise continued. It seemed to be parallel to
him. It was then that the apprehension Dan had felt earlier
came sweeping over him like a wave. Only this time the feeling cut through him like a knife. A shiver started in the small
of his back. By the time it climbed the length of his spinal column, his entire body shook. At the same time the now
unwanted companion moved onto the road directly to Dan's
right and seemed to measure its stride against Dan's. Without
changing his cadence, Dan's head naturally turned in its direction. But darkness prevailed, and he could see nothing of the
intruder. Instinctively he reached for the flashlight in the hol-
ster that he wore on his hip. But sensing that whatever it was
that walked next to him was of good size, he knew that star-
tling it with the light could prove dangerous if it panicked. So
the senior scout decided to forego the light in favor of calming
himself and regaining control of his fear.

The sound of its footsteps seemed to ring in the young
man's ears. Its breathing was heavy and coarse, almost raspy. A
bitter, somewhat rancid odor, much like that of a damp,
unkempt animal, filled the air. Dan wouldn't even try to tell
you that he was without concern, but somehow he did man-
age to remain somewhat calm. He tried to maintain his pace
as best he could, although maybe somewhat quicker. Dan held
his head rigidly straight ahead. He could feel that his body
was tight with tension. The urge to bolt was almost overwhelming. Somehow he managed to resist this urge and maintain his now quickened pace.

Now I agree that it may sound strange, but Dan found

himself curious as to exactly what his new-found companion was—or wasn't! His fear gave way, at least momentarily, to curiosity. He began to try to decipher what the creature was that walked next to him. The possibility that it was human was quickly dismissed. By the smell, it could have been a large fur-bearing animal, possibly damp from crossing a stream. But then it should have hoofs, which, on the hard road, would make a clip-clop sound. It was then that Dan listened to its footsteps, and then his apprehension came flying back! There was definitely clipping noises, which would mean hoofs—but there were no clops from hind legs! With bated breath, the young man strained his ears, trying to hear more than two legs. Dan's mouth became dry, his breathing short and gasping. He wondered if the thing could sense the terror that now possessed every cell in his body.

The senior scout wasn't sure how much farther he had to go until he came into the light of the main campground. At this time panic seemed to take over, and Dan quickened his pace dramatically. To his horror, so did his invisible companion. It stayed directly to the right. Dan's heart felt as if it would pound right through his chest. Dan's breathing was very short and gaspy, almost to the point of hyperventilation. Suddenly it occurred to him that its breathing had changed. It was now short and deep, sort of a snorting, as if it had become aggravated. The young man's terror was now complete. It is uncertain what would have happened if Dan hadn't seen the light of the main camp shining through the woods ahead of him. The light at least gave him some hope, which didn't deter the fear so much as allow Dan to control it somewhat. The scout concentrated on the light and quickened the pace to a near run. Dan could feel that the enigma had kept pace and remained at his side. Its breathing becoming louder as the pace became faster. Dan could see the light on the road ahead and focused his mind on the fact that he would be safe if he could only make it to the light. With only a few yards to go, his terror-ridden strides were more like leaps. His heart was pounding so hard Dan was sure it would jump from his chest. His lungs burned with each gasped breath. Dan found himself urging his body along. Then with only a matter of steps to go . . . all became silent . . . except for his labored breathing and the sound of his footsteps. Dan continued on until he was well into the lighted section of the road. He then stopped and spun around. Dan was sure it was till there in the middle of the road. He was sure that he hadn't heard the creature move off to the side. He stared at the darkness, almost expecting it to suddenly leap out at him, but somehow knowing that it wouldn't . Dan reached for his flashlight and aimed it back down the road. Gritting his teeth to maintain his courage, Dan turned it on!

There was nothing there! The senior scout swung the light quickly back and forth, but still there was nothing. Dan stood for sometime, breathing heavily and shining the light down the road. Finally he went on to the shower house and tried to soothe his jagged nerves with a very hot, very long shower. As he stood there with the water running over his lowered head, curiosity took over where only moments before there was only fear and terror.

"Why didn't I shine my light on it sooner?" he asked himself, "at least I would have seen it. I would have known what it was!" Dan became angry and chastised himself for being such a coward.

Then it occurred to him that he still had to go back to

camp, and that he might encounter it again. All he had to do was walk back in the dark just as he had come. Surely it would still be there. Dan literally jumped from the shower and dressed. With his hair still wet, the troop's senior patrol leader headed back to camp.

But Dan never saw it again. To this day he still has no idea what it was. Every now and then he thinks about it, usually while walking the woods at night. He's still curious as to what it could have been. Dan didn't get to see it on his way back to camp that night. Of course, he knew he wouldn't if he had a light on. He had a very good light; he'd just put new batteries in it that day. Dan figures they burned out . . . sometime before dawn.

# STORY OUTLINE

I.      After the troop was settled for the night, the senior patrol leader, Dan Livingston, left for the main campground to take a shower.

II.      Walking along the pitch-black road, Dan suddenly noticed that the woods had become quieter than before.

III.      The feeling of apprehension was intensified when he became aware of a sudden rustling noise along the side of the road.

IV.      A shiver of fear started in the small of his back and climbed the length of his spinal column as the unwanted companion moved onto the road directly to his right and seemed to take up his stride.

V.    He looked in the direction of the noise but could see nothing of the intruder in the inky blackness of the night.

VI.    He instinctively reached for his flashlight, but he hesitated using it for fear that he might startle the creature, which could prove dangerous if it panicked.

VII.    The creature's breathing was heavy, and the odor of a damp animal filled the air.

VIII.    As Dan tensely walked on, he struggled to keep his speed even.

IX.    He tried to imagine what sort of creature was walking alongside him in the dark.

X.    His ears strained to study the footsteps of the animal—he heard a clipping noise of hoofs, but no clops from hind legs.

XI.    Terribly frightened, he quickened his pace—and so did his nighttime companion.

XII.    The creature started snorting, as if aggravated by the quickened pace.

XIII.    The light of the main camp became visible in the distance, providing Dan some hope.

XIV.    The scout concentrated on the light and quickened his pace to a near run.

XV.     The creature kept pace—Dan breathed in gasps and his heart pounded as he ran desperately for the safety of the main camp.

XVI.    With only steps to go, Dan suddenly realized the only sound he heard was his own labored breathing.

XVII.   He stopped and spun around. Seeing nothing, he aimed his flashlight and turned it on. . . . There was nothing there!

XVIII.  At first relieved, Dan's curiosity increased; he became angry with himself because he had not shined his light on the creature to learn its identity.

XIX.    He left the shower and eagerly looked forward to the adventure of returning to camp.

XX.     But he never saw the creature. Of course, he knew that he would not see it if he used his flashlight—and his flashlight probably did not burn itself out until nearly dawn.

# THE MINNESOTA MAGGOT
# OF DEATH

as told by William Forgey

*This old folk tale is simple, yet it readily conjures up thoughts of an evil and hideous ghoulie—one that becomes particularly dreadful around a campfire, deep in the woods on some dark night. Try to personalize the introduction, much as I have.*

During a recent visit to my old canoe buddy, Cliff Jacobson, I was shown an overgrown church cemetery hear his hometown of Hastings, Minnesota. Perhaps the most loathsome and terrifying apparition ever seen there was a maggoty creature that was said to have haunted this little Minnesota churchyard years ago.

The first man to see it was Mr. Thomas, the baker. He was passing the graveyard on his way home on a bright moonlit night when his attention was caught by a large blob of luminous ooze, issuing from the fresh grave of a recently dead villager names Jenkins. The giant, ugly glowworm wriggled and grew bigger as it slithered from the ground. Repulsed and horrified, Thomas was nevertheless fascinated by the creature. It looked exactly like a giant glowing maggot. He never liked cutting through the cemetery by himself, so it took all of the courage that he could muster to even watch the monster. When he saw its eyes, he was forced to look away from the creature, for the evil creature stared in a strangely human fashion. Its hideous face seemed to recognize him, yet it was decidedly not human—it was a creature from beyond the grave that exuded pure evil.

Thomas followed the ghastly monster as it slithered along the ground, leaving a gleaming trail of disgusting slime in its wake. The maggot wriggled along the paths between the tombstones and soon reached the edge of the graveyard. Thomas followed the slimy trail until it ended at the door of the village postmaster's house nearby.

The next day Thomas told his wife and his best friend

about the incredible experience. That night the three of them went to the cemetery to see if they could discover anything more about the hideous monster. Suddenly the ground above Jenkins's grave quivered and the dreadful creature oozed forth. The three friends followed at a distance until it disappeared once again at the postmaster's house. The next day the Thomases and their friend were shocked to learn that the postmaster and his entire family had taken ill. Worse, by the time the sun set that night, all members of the family were dead. The perplexed doctor taking care of them decided that they had all died of carbon monoxide poisoning.

Resolved now more than ever to learn about the glowing maggot's origin, Thomas, his wife, and their friend returned to the grave that very night. Again the ground above Jenkins's grave trembled and the glowing maggot poked its slimy head above the surface. The creature slithered up from the grave, glanced in their direction, and then crawled between the tombstones. Following the familiar trail of glowing slime, the three friends followed the trail until it vanished at the house of the village school principal. There was no need for the creature to visit the principal a second time, nor did Thomas have a chance to warn him. The principal became ill in the morning and died before sunset, like the postmaster and his family, of carbon monoxide poisoning.

Now completely frightened and more bewildered than ever, Thomas and his companions decided to return to the graveyard that very night. Almost to their astonishment, nothing happened. They were afraid to tell anyone of their sightings for fear that they would be made to look hysterical or even implicated in the deaths. They decided to maintain their nightly vigil at the grave for at least two weeks.

On the tenth night of watching, the creature again emerged from Jenkins's grave, this time slithering purposefully straight toward the Thomas home. The Thomases were horror stricken. Rushing in to their house, they grabbed their five-year-old son and rushed him outside. That night they all stayed at their friend's house. In the morning they found their pet dog, Jack, dead—the vet said of carbon monoxide poisoning.

That very night, their hearts filled with anger and fear, Thomas and his wife, accompanied by their friend, went back to the grave site. This time they meant to strike back at the monster. Equipped with a kerosene lantern and shovels, they dug up the grave of the last Mr. Jenkins.

When they struck the coffin, Mrs. Thomas held the lantern, while her husband and his friend pried the lid off. Mrs. Thomas shrieked when she saw the corpse, dropping her lantern. Mr. Thomas and his friend sprang back from the coffin allowing the lid to slam shut, but before it closed, they could both see that a hideous green glow emanated from it.

The two men then placed a rope around the coffin and dragged it from the graveyard to a nearby field. Taking the now broken lantern, they poured the remaining kerosene over the coffin and lit it on fire burning it to cinders. After returning to the cemetery, they filled the grave and covered all traces of their having been there.

The monstrous maggot of death was never seen again. Mr. Thomas later learned that the dead man had been on bad terms with both the postmaster and the school principal. He had never had any trouble with Jenkins, but he remembered with a shutter how the evil glowing maggot had stared at him as it crawled away from the cemetery on its way to perform its hideous deeds.

# STORY OUTLINE

I.     Mr. Thomas was passing through the cemetery one night when he saw a hideous blob of luminous ooze wriggle up from a fresh grave.

II.     A glowing, monstrous maggot slithered out of the graveyard, leaving a trail of gleaming slime until it disappeared into the postmaster's house.

III.     Mr. Thomas, his wife, and best friend returned to the grave the next night, and again the glowing maggot slithered from the cemetery to the postmaster's house.

IV.     The next day the postmaster and his entire family took ill and were dead by sunset—the doctor felt from carbon monoxide poisoning.

V.     The three companions returned to the churchyard the following night and again watched as the glowing maggot left the grave and made its way to the school principal's house.

VI.     The school principal became ill in the morning and died before the three friends could warn him. Carbon monoxide poisoning was also said to be the cause of the principal's death.

VII. Thoroughly alarmed, yet afraid to look foolish to the authorities, Mr. Thomas and his companions watched the cemetery nightly, but nothing happened for ten days.

VIII. When it reappeared, the glowing maggot headed directly for the Thomas house. Terrified, they took their son and spent the night at their friend's home.

IX. On returning home they found that their pet dog, which had been left behind in their haste, was dead—the vet said from carbon monoxide poisoning.

X. That night the three friends returned to the graveyard and dug up the corpse from Jenkin's grave.

XI. They removed the coffin to a nearby field and burned it to cinders.

XII. They learned that the dead man had hated the postmaster and school principal. He had never had any trouble with Jenkins, but Thomas remembered with a shutter how the evil glowing maggot had stared at him as it crawled away from the cemetery on its way to perform its hideous deeds.

# About the Author

William W. "Doc" Forgey, M.D. is an outdoorsman and physician from Gary, Indiana. He has been telling ghost stories for years to children and adults. He honed his storytelling skills during his ten years as a scout leader and on canoeing and camping trips with friends.

In addition to telling tales, William Forgey is the editor of *Campfire Stories volume 1* and *volume 3*, and is the author of *Wilderness Medicine, Basic Essentials: First Aid,* and *Basic Essentials: Hypothermia,* all published by The Globe Pequot Press. He is also a member of the Northern Tier High Adventure Base Committee for the Boy Scouts of America, a member of the scouts' National Health and Safety Committee, and is President of the Wilderness Medical Society.

Finally, he wants to reassure parents that scary stories are fun and are *not* detrimental to children's health!